TEAM REAPER THRILLERS

RETRIBUTION
DEADLY INTENT
TERMINATION ORDER
BLOOD RUSH
KILL COUNT
RELENTLESS
LETHAL TENDER
EMPTY QUIVER
BARRACUDA!
AFRICAN WHITE
KILL THEORY
DANGER CLOSE
COLLATERAL DAMAGE

KANE: TOOTH & NAIL
KANE: CENTER MASS
KANE: DARKNESS UPON US
KANE: DEEP BLACK

KANE: BORN OF THE REAPER

FEAR THE REAPER 5

BRENT TOWNS

ROUGH
EDGES
PRESS

**ROUGH
EDGES
PRESS**

Published in the United States by Wolfpack Publishing, Las Vegas

Rough Edges Press
An Imprint of Wolfpack Publishing
5130 S. Fort Apache Rd. 215-380
Las Vegas, NV 89148

roughedgespress.com

Paperback ISBN: 978-1-68549-076-8
eBook ISBN: 978-1-68549-075-1
LCCN: 2022934839

KANE: BORN OF THE REAPER

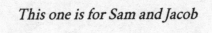
This one is for Sam and Jacob

KOWLOON, HONG KONG
PRESENT DAY...

John 'Reaper' Kane felt the hair on the back of his neck stand up. Something wasn't right, he could feel it. The neon lights of the city shone bright against an inky night sky. Concrete and glass skyscrapers reached up into the darkness like fingers trying to touch Heaven.

Kane checked his watch. It was almost midnight. He'd been in position to meet his contact for the past thirty-minutes, but the person was a no-show.

MI6 had reached out to his commander, former general Mary Thurston, asking if they could 'borrow' him for a small mission to Hong Kong. When she pressed for additional information, was told that Kane had been requested specifically.

As with any off-team activities, Thurston had left the decision up to him, and the big former Recon Marine, his interest piqued, decided to take the job.

Before leaving RAF Brize Norton, he'd been briefed by an MI6 officer named Welsh.

"You'll go to Hong Kong and meet your contact there. They will then take you to meet the person of interest."

"Why me?" Kane asked.

Welsh had shrugged. "I don't know."

"What do I do when I meet this person?"

"You'll stay with them in an undisclosed location until we can arrange to get you out."

"I'm guessing this person is Chinese?"

"American chap actually. Once worked for some covert CIA unit in Vietnam back in the day. Someone is trying to kill him, so he came to us for protection. Then he asked for you."

"And you don't know why?"

"Not a clue, old chap."

It was then that they'd flown him to Hong Kong.

Now, at the meeting spot, something wasn't right.

In the hollow of his lower back, Kane could feel the reassuring pressure of his SIG Sauer P226 handgun. Stepping casually into the shadows offered by one of the large buildings, it would appear that he had simply vanished, if anyone were observing him.

Which is exactly what those who were watching him thought had happened. Three men, all Asian in appearance, materialized from an alley across the street. All were armed with QBZ-95 Bullpup assault rifles.

What the hell were these guys doing with assault rifles in the middle of Kowloon?

Gripping the P226 tight in his fist, he waited for them to cross the street. As soon as they placed their feet on the sidewalk, he stepped clear of the shadows and said, "Are you guys looking for me?"

A flurry of words from the middle man was quickly followed by all three starting to lift their weapons.

However, before they could bring them into a firing position, the P226 was operational, and the first man had two rounds in his chest.

Kane shifted his aim and planted two in the second guy's chest just as he was ready to fire his weapon.

The third attacker managed to fire a burst that flew wide before Kane put him down. Three bodies lying on the sidewalk, with not a movement from any of them.

The man they called the Reaper looked around, checking the immediate surroundings for any additional attackers who might walk up on him. When he was satisfied there weren't, he hurried forward to check the dead men over.

He was not surprised to find them clean of any identifiers apart from the tattoo each one had on his right wrist. It was a scorpion that Kane had never seen before.

The sound of a footfall on concrete brought Kane to his feet, his weapon sweeping around in the direction of the noise. Standing before him, wearing a long coat, his hands in the pockets, was a man. "Who are you?" Kane snarled.

"I'm the man you were sent to meet," came the posh reply.

"You're a bit fucking late."

"You handled yourself rather well. I can see that the rumors are true."

"Who are you?" Kane asked again, this time his tone was more forceful.

"Tim Roberts."

"Uh, huh. Who are these guys?"

"Kowloon Triad. They're marked by the scorpion tattoos."

Kane nodded. "I saw them."

Sirens sounded in the distance. Roberts said, "Unless you want to end up in a Chinese prison, I suggest you come with me."

Kane followed the man along the street and then into an alley, only looking back twice. Halfway down the alley, they came to a black Range Rover which Roberts unlocked and suggested that they not tarry. As Roberts pulled away from the curb, Kane asked, "You have any idea what that was about?"

"Not entirely but the triad is trying to kill our mutual friend as well as yourself, it would seem."

"The question is," Kane replied, "how did they know I was coming?"

Roberts glanced at Kane and said, "Add it to the list."

***

"We're here," Roberts said as he eased the Range Rover to a stop.

Kane looked out the window and then back at the fair-haired MI6 officer. "This is your safehouse?"

"Is there something wrong with it?" Roberts asked as he opened his door.

"It's a frigging fifty-floor five-star hotel," Kane pointed out incredulously.

"I'm well aware of what it is. What better place to hide a valuable person?"

"But how is he valuable?"

"Come inside and I'll tell you."

As they climbed out, the valet approached and

handed Roberts a ticket in exchange for the keys of the Rover. They went in through large double glass doors, and instantly Kane was struck by the décor. The floor was a red marble with a high luster, the reception counter was a polished mahogany. There were numerous oil paintings in oversized gilt frames adorning the walls, and stands of lush greenery, palms and leafy tropical plants, dotted the foyer itself. People came and went even though the hour was just before midnight.

"Over here," Roberts said, and led the way toward a bank of elevators.

Once inside, Roberts pressed the button for the 42nd floor and turned to Kane. "Our friend upstairs worked for the CIA in Vietnam at the time of the war. He has information pertaining to the Kowloon Triad which is quickly becoming the largest organized crime syndicate in Hong Kong. He has agreed to help us take them down, but in doing so, he asked that we find you first."

"Why?"

"I don't know."

"All right, answer me this. Why is MI6 getting mixed up in a drug operation?"

"The triad's drugs have started flooding British shores. The problem is, they've done something to it which has made it substantially more addictive than anything we've ever seen before. The worst part is that when the addicts are coming down from a high, they get violent. Crime rates, including drug associated murders, have gone through the roof."

When they reached the desired floor, the elevator pinged, and the doors opened. They stepped out into a long, carpeted hallway, and Roberts instructed Kane to turn left. They had passed four rooms before Roberts told him to stop, then opened the door with an electronic key.

On the other side of the door waiting for them to enter, armed with an MP5, was a young woman dressed in a pants suit. Roberts said, "Is everything all right?"

"Yes, fine." She looked Kane up and down. "Is this the blighter we're waiting for?"

"It is. John Kane, meet Sara Harris."

"Pleasure, ma'am."

"Likewise, I'm sure."

She led them into a large living area where a man was sitting on a long sofa, watching an old black and white western. He looked up at Kane and said, "Four Fast Guns, son. A western classic."

Kane nodded. "I've seen it. My grandfather loved that movie."

The man gave him a solemn look. "I know, son. I know."

Kane frowned. The man was somewhere in his late seventies. Maybe even early eighties. His white hair had thinned some over the years. "You knew my grandfather?"

"Sure did, son, back in Vietnam and some after. Good man, great man was the Reaper."

Kane stared at him warily. "What's your name?"

The old man shrugged. "What's in a name? Today it's one thing, tomorrow it's different."

"Just tell him, Calvin," Sara chided him.

The old man sighed. "Calvin Stuart. That's my name. Back in the day though I went by so many I'm not even sure if Cal is my right one."

"What did my grandfather call you?"

"Called me whatever the hell he wanted to."

"Why did you want to see me?" Kane asked.

"I heard about you, son."

Kane was confused. "What?"

"Yes, sir. Tough son of a bitch. Well, you'll need to be."

"What do you mean?"

"To get the ones responsible for killing old Reaper."

"My grandfather died in a plane crash in ninety-five," Kane said.

Stuart's eyes narrowed and his voice grew harsh. "Your grandfather was murdered, son. That's why I'm here. I want you to know the truth about everything so you can deal out some of that justice of yours."

Kane was stunned. He'd always thought the whole plane thing was an accident. That's what the report said. But here was this guy he didn't know telling him that his grandfather, the man Kane had been named after, had been murdered. "How do I know you're speaking the truth?" Kane asked him.

Stuart reached into his coat pocket and took out a small, well-worn book. He handed it to Kane and said, "Take a seat, son. It's all in there. Your grandfather kept a diary from the start to the end. When you're done, I'll do my best to answer anything you want to know."

CAMBODIA, 1968...

Duke stopped. Just froze on the spot and lowered himself to the jungle floor beneath the triple canopy above. It was the fourth time he'd done it since they'd left their camp that morning. Each time it had been a precautionary halt. This time, when the Vietnamese scout turned to face me, I could tell by his expression that something was wrong.

"VC! VC!" he whispered urgently.

My broad shoulders stiffened. Everything was VC to our indigenous Montagnard scouts, Duke, Jimmy, Audie, and Scotty. We couldn't say their names, so we gave them nicknames instead after the great western stars of the 50s and early 60s. Not one of them was older than nineteen. Just kids. But each was good at their job which was why the Military Assistance Command Vietnam-Studies and Observations Group (MACV-SOG) utilized them. If ever I had to rely on them in a fight, I was confident they would be front and center.

Behind me I felt the presence of my second in command, One-One, Corporal Marty Willis. He eased down beside me and asked, "What is it, Reaper?"

I turned slowly and looked at him. His face was black from the cammo paint he'd rubbed on it before we had climbed onto the UH-1 Huey and left our FOB or forward operating base two days before on our mission. That all went to shit when the team I was One-Zero of and commander, callsign ST Denver, was asked to take a stroll across the Cambodian border to 'take a peek' at a suspected VC camp. Ever since, we'd been playing hide and seek with enemy patrols. This was dangerous work. Teams were known to have simply vanished off the face of the earth after being inserted. "Duke says there's VC ahead of us."

"Again?" the big dark-haired Montanan said skeptically. "I'm starting to think the jungle is getting the better of him."

Not only was Marty my One-One, he was also my radio man, and the AN/PRC 25 radio kept us in touch with the outside world via our forward air controller or Covey.

Behind him came Jack, my One-Two, and then Billy Smith, my One-Three. All were seasoned Special Forces men and well trained in jungle tactics. Behind Billy came the rest of the scouts.

Whenever we went out, we went clean. No identifying tags or shit like that. We carried our weapons and extra ammo along with grenades and claymores.

I studied the jungle ahead of us, sweat dripping down from my nose. The humidity beneath the canopy was getting worse and I was looking forward to the afternoon storms to clear the air some. My grip tightened on my CAR-15. All the indigenous scouts were similarly armed. Jack, however, carried an M79 grenade launcher, or thumper, and Billy a pump-action shotgun with the barrel cut short. Ever since he'd been in country, Billy figured that the shotgun was more conducive to him staying alive in the close confines of the jungle. Marty, on the other hand, also carried a CAR-15.

I crept forward to where Duke still squatted. "What's wrong?"

"VC! Beaucoup VC."

I turned to stare at Marty and signaled him to get everyone off the trail we were using. They disappeared into the slick undergrowth, and then I turned back to Duke. Not for the first time that day the cloying humidity felt as though it was trying to suffocate me. "Let's go have a look."

We moved forward at a speed which would have seen a tortoise outpace us. One thing you learned when running missions in the jungle: speed meant death.

For twenty minutes we crept forward through the thick undergrowth, gently pushing branches away. I felt confident that Marty would be setting up the rest of the team into a defensive position with claymore mines ready to use around the small perimeter. Claymores, we never left home without them. More than once, they'd saved my life and those of my team.

By the time we found the enemy, it felt as though we'd gone two klicks farther along when in fact it was no more than one hundred meters.

"See, Boss," Duke said nervously.

He'd been right to be nervous. We'd found the VC. Except it was NVA. North Vietnamese Army regulars. It looked to be a basecamp set up for a raiding party to slip across the border that night. If it hadn't been for Duke, we would have blundered right into them. My best estimates had them at about forty combatants. It could have been more. Too many for us to be dicing with.

I touched Duke on the shoulder. "Keep an eye on them. I'm going back to call it in."

He shook his head. "No, no. We go."

"Duke—"

"No, we go."

I could see by the expression on his face it was no good. Maybe Marty was right. Maybe he'd been at it too long. I nodded. "All right, come on."

We started making our way back to the others, moving as silently as before, me keeping one eye on Duke as we proceeded. However, it wasn't the scout I should have worried about.

The jungle ahead of us came alive with the sound of gunfire. The crack of automatic weapons and then the recognizable sound of the shotgun and grenade launcher.

"Fuck it," I hissed tersely. "Come on, Duke."

Already I could hear the NVA behind us shouting at each other. "Wait," I snapped. "Watch that way," I ordered Duke, pointing towards the direction the team was.

The scout lowered himself to his knee and waited nervously while I pulled a claymore from my pack. I poked it into the jungle floor and set the fuse. "Let's go," I barked coming to my feet.

We started off again but this time we left the trail and headed into the jungle, all the while I was counting off the seconds in my mind. The claymore went up with a roar.

I never waited to see what would happen after that. I just kept Duke moving forward until we regrouped with the others

***

"What frigging happened?" I demanded as Marty reloaded his CAR-15 with a fresh mag.

"Fucking patrol crept up on us."

"We'll talk about this later. Set the fuses on those claymores and we'll get the fuck out of here."

The jungle exploded around us, then we were up and moving, deeper into the undergrowth away from the trail.

I kept them going for ten minutes, Jimmy on point with Jack, while Audie and Scotty pulled rear security.

We stopped and sucked in deep breaths. Sweat ran off us in rivers. "Marty, call it in." I continued by saying, "Tell him we've just broken contact with a large force of NVA and are making for anywhere that will fit a damned helo. Shit! Fuck! Tell him some air support—"

BOOM!

I ducked my head. Now they were firing mortars. "Tell Jollyman we need air support for extract."

I looked at the others. "Check ammo. Set up a perimeter."

We remained in that position until Marty had finished on the radio. He looked at me. "Jollyman is relaying the message. He's coming further in and will remain on station until we're picked up."

I grabbed my map from inside my pocket. I unfolded it and looked it over, stabbing at it with a grime-stained finger. "Here. We make this our primary LZ. Call it in."

"Looks good to me," Marty agreed.

"All right, let's move."

We changed direction to the south and the new landing zone. Once again, I had the men slow their pace to save stumbling into another armed force. The day wore on, the sun growing lower in the sky and the dappled light below the canopy became darker. It was now that I realized we weren't going to make the LZ before nightfall.

"Marty, come here with the radio. Jack, set up another perimeter."

Marty settled down beside me and gave me the radio handset. "Jollyman, Jollyman this is Delta One-Zero, over."

"Read you five by five Delta One-Zero. What's your status, over?"

"We're still ahead in the game, Jollyman. But we're not going to reach the primary LZ before dark. Once the weather closes in, we'll be fucked. Over."

"Copy, One-Zero. Will turn the birds around and remain on station to put you to bed, over."

"Copy, Jollyman. One-Zero out."

I turned to Marty. "We'll keep moving until dark then call it a day. Do we have any claymores left?"

"A couple."

"That's something."

"Be good to be drinking beer about now, Reaper."

"Ain't that the truth. Let's keep moving."

We walked for another two hours, most of that

through pouring rain, before I called a halt.

"Jollyman, this is Delta One-Zero, over."

"This is Jollyman, One-Zero. Read you loud and clear. Over."

"We're calling it a night, over. See you in the morning. One-Zero out."

"Take care."

"You too, Jollyman."

It was kept short, for the NVA, it was reported, had good direction-finding capabilities.

As we lay there in silence in a wagon wheel formation, I thought I could hear the Cessna O-2 Skymaster in the distance as it left station. Marty put out the remaining two claymores and then came back in.

"How's it look?"

"Quiet as a church."

"I'll take first watch with Duke," I told him for the simple reason, I still didn't trust Duke after what I'd seen earlier in the day.

"All right. Wake me when you're ready to swap."

"Copy that."

***

The night passed quietly and the following morning I sent Marty and Jimmy out for a look around and to retrieve the claymores. They returned thirty minutes later, reporting all clear. With that done I reached for the handset of the radio.

"Jollyman, Jollyman, this is Delta One-Zero, over."

I waited and then tried again. "Jollyman, Jollyman, Jollyman, this is Delta One-Zero, over."

"Delta One-Zero this is Jollyman. Read you loud

and clear, over."

I gave the FAC an update and then said, "We'll be moving in the next five mikes, over."

"Copy that, One-Zero. Will have your ride spin up and see if I can get some gunships to cover the extract. Jollyman out."

I crawled over to where Audie sat. "You go on point."

The young man gave me a confident smile. "No problem."

He slipped out into the jungle and started towards the primary LZ where we would be picked up. However, between us and the LZ was a creek crossing and two low ridges which we would have to negotiate.

Jack Lynch followed Audie into the jungle, and I followed him. My thinking was that if Audie should run into trouble, then the M79 would act as a kind of deterrent. We moved slowly and an hour later, without incident, we reached the creek crossing.

Audie started to make his way into the narrow strip of water. It came up to his waist as he waded across. He emerged on the far bank and knelt on the ground. Without looking back, he motioned Lynch to follow him.

However, I stopped Jack and motioned to Billy to go. The big man from Kentucky began making his way across the creek. He made it out the other side without any problems.

Next, I motioned to Duke. He still had a nervous look in his eyes from the day before. He only made it halfway before the jungle all around erupted in gunfire.

Duke took a round to his chest. I didn't know it at

the time, but he was already dying even though I was trying to get to the creek to pull him in. However, Marty grabbed me and dragged me to the ground.

"Get the fuck down, Reaper," he snarled at me. "He's done. Just like we all will be if we can't regroup."

He was right. "We need to get them back from across the creek. Jack, put some cover down with the M79! Set up a perimeter."

No sooner had the words left my mouth when I saw Billy dragging Audie behind him. The big Kentuckian stopped at the edge of the creek and let Audie go. He then cut loose with his shotgun as an enemy soldier emerged from the jungle in front of him.

In the time that this had happened, Lynch had fired two M79 grenades into the jungle beyond them. If there were any NVA in there, they were no longer.

I dropped out an empty mag from my CAR-15. Reloaded with a fresh one and started to spray the jungle on full auto.

Marty came in beside me and did the same. While Scotty and Jimmy watched our rear.

"Billy, move!" I shouted at him. He let go another two rounds and started to pull Audie across the creek with him. All this time I hadn't noticed but the Yard still had his weapon.

Two NVA soldiers appeared at the edge of the creek. I sprayed one with a burst of fire while Marty got the other. I grabbed for a grenade on my webbing and threw it as far as I could. It landed in the undergrowth and exploded savagely.

Meanwhile heavy fire was still coming our way and vegetation fell as though cut down by an invisible scythe. I threw another grenade and shouted to Marty, "Get Covey on the horn. Tell him we need air support, now."

By some miracle, Billy managed to get Audie back across the creek. Now that we were back together, I gave the order to set up a decent perimeter. Both myself and Billy covered the creek crossing while the others set up in a wagon wheel formation.

"Reaper, air support is five mikes out," my One-One called to me.

I dropped out another magazine and reloaded once more, glad that I'd ordered everyone to bring extra ammo on this trip. I fired at another NVA soldier who jerked and fell face first into the creek. I glanced over at Audie who though wounded, had joined the fight.

Suddenly an explosion erupted from the creek. The bastards had mortars. I could hear the whistles urging the enemy on and had a bad feeling that we'd stumbled on a regiment. Most likely the ones from the day before.

"Marty!"

He crawled over to me.

"What?"

"Get ready to move. We can't wait for the air."

"We can't go with Audie," Marty informed me. "He's hit in a leg. He won't make it."

"Fuck," I hissed. "Get me the radio."

As bullets snapped close overhead, I called Covey. "Jollyman, Jollyman, this is Delta One-Zero, over."

"Read you loud and clear, One-Zero, over."

"I'm declaring a Prairie Fire emergency, over."

"Say again, One-Zero."

"Prairie Fire, Jollyman. I'm declaring a Prairie

Fire emergency."

"Roger, One-Zero, you're declaring a Prairie fire emergency."

A Prairie fire emergency was declared when the SOG unit on the ground was about to be overrun and was in a desperate way. Next step was a call would go out and every available aircraft would be scrambled to assist. While back at base a Bright Light team would be put on standby should it be needed.

I dropped the handset and sprayed the jungle once more with heavy fire before throwing out another grenade. I felt bullets tug at my clothing but dismissed it. A cry of pain drew my attention and I saw Billy grabbing at his upper arm. "Billy, are you alright?"

"Don't fucking worry about me. Keep the pricks back."

For the next few minutes, we burned through our ammo and the last of our grenades. Jack had no more rounds left for the M79, and although wounded, Billy was holding his own along with Audie.

I picked up the handset again. "Jollyman, Jollyman, this is Delta One-Zero, over."

"Roger, One-Zero. We have air support inbound, over."

"Copy, Jollyman."

I grabbed a smoke cannister out of my pack and tossed it a few feet in front of our position. Red smoke started to rise through the jungle. I hadn't advertised the fact over the radio because the NVA had intercept capability and they also carried smoke with them to fool the air assets.

Jollyman came back to me. "Delta One-Zero I see

red smoke. I say again, I see red smoke, over."

"Roger, Jollyman. I need the assets to do bomb and gun runs from north to south, over."

"Roger, One-Zero. Keep your heads down."

Within moments I could hear the first of the helicopter gunships coming in above the jungle. Soon miniguns opened fire and shredded everything in the top of the canopy. The rounds were like scythes chopping the shit out of it. It wasn't long before large patches of light filtered through.

Still, all around us muzzle flashes could be seen. If we were to get to our LZ then I needed to have our front on the other side of the creek cleared. Another two gunships came in and copied the actions of the first. I tossed the handset to Marty. "Guide the rest of them in while I check on Audie."

I crawled over to the wounded Yard. "How you doing, Buddy?"

"Hurt like bitch," he growled. As he rolled onto his back to reload, I checked his leg. It looked as though the bullet had gone right through.

"You'll live."

Suddenly Marty called out. "Everyone duck, Skyraiders coming in with Napalm."

Just what we needed. A couple of Douglas A-1 Skyraiders with a load of Napalm, a gasoline jelly agent which exploded into a rolling fireball and was pure hell to see coming at you.

A wall of flame rose on the other side of the creek. We hugged the earth just in case the pilot was off target, but these guys were good at their job and by the time the second plane had completed its run, the jungle opposite us was a blackened mess.

"Hey, boss," Marty called to me. "Jollyman says

he's got two Super Sabres up top. Where do you want it?"

We were still taking fire from the east, so I called back to put it there. Within moments, the call had been relayed and the first F-100 jet made its run. Like the Skyraiders, the Super Sabres had Napalm and soon the jungle to the east was burning also.

"Reaper, we've got problems," Marty said to me. "They're going for a STABO rig extraction. Charlie has reinforcements coming in from the north and east."

"How long?"

"Five mikes."

"All right, everyone, get ready."

A STABO rig required the guys on the ground to strap on a harness; the extracting helicopter would drop a rope and the troops on the ground would hook onto it. The helicopter would then lift, taking the soldiers clear of the jungle and then fly away. That's the way it was supposed to work. I'd heard stories of SF guys getting hooked up in trees and others falling out of the harness because they weren't strapped in them properly. Not something you want to do at a couple of thousand feet.

With the lull that the Napalm brought us we were able to get ready for extraction as the gunships made another run.

Then came the call from the extract bird. "Delta One-Zero this is Zulu One, we're coming in."

"Roger, Zulu One."

The sound of the helicopter overhead was a welcome one indeed. While it came down, I noticed Billy run down to the creek. I frowned then realized what he was doing. He was getting Duke. No man left behind.

The rope came down and next thing we were hauling ass out of there up through what was left of the triple canopy, all the while taking rounds from the ground.

***

The one rule when you're operating with SOG is that you don't talk about SOG. That was why we signed non-disclosure documents. Hell, not even military personnel knew about SOG. We did things that other people knew nothing about. Whole recon teams disappeared, and the official word was KIA. That was it, nothing else.

We debriefed upon our arrival back at base and then were told we could have a few days R&R. Which, after running missions for the past month, was a welcome relief.

So we went to Mama San's. A strip joint full of willing girls and drunk GIs. We sat at a table, Billy, Jack, Marty, and me. The beer was warm and tasted like piss, but it was wet, and no one gave two fucks about it. Jack stared at the dancers on the stage while Billy sat there with his head back looking at the ceiling. Partially hidden under the table was a local stripper using her mouth to good effect to earn an extra couple of dollars.

I sat and toyed with my beer while Marty was already on his way to being drunk. The man fought hard and drank harder. He held up his beer bottle and said, "Fuck 'em all."

I picked up my beer and held it aloft. "Amen to that."

The sound of a table crashing across the room

brought raised voices. Two drunken GIs rose to their feet, swinging wildly trying to hit each other but missing by feet. Their friends calmed them down and they resumed their seats.

I saw another GI sucking on a stick of hooch while a dark-haired beauty gyrated on his lap. Blinking I realized she didn't have any pants on, and I assumed the GI wasn't wearing any either.

A young lady came over to me and grinned. "You want fuck, Joe?"

I shook my head. "No, I'm good."

"I do," Billy said.

She pointed at the head bobbing up and down on his lap. "You already got one."

"I want another one," he growled and got to his feet.

The young lady who'd been working between his legs looked disappointed. "You not finish yet."

He picked her up with one arm. "Come on, Baby, I'm not finished with you."

They moved off through the crowd toward the back area of the bar where the cribs were. I didn't expect to see Billy before dawn now.

Jack sighed and took a sip of his beer. "You got plans?" I asked him.

He turned his head, staring at me bleary eyed. "Yeah, I'm going to get drunk, have a sleep, and do it all over again."

"Sounds like a good plan."

"What about you, Reaper?"

I shrugged. "Don't know. Maybe I might find me a game somewhere."

"Yeah, right."

We sat silently and had another beer each. R&R had suddenly become boring. But not for long.

Entering the bar was a man wearing the uniform of an army major. Major bullshit, he had CIA written all over him. I tracked him with my eyes as he walked to the bar to order a beer. Two dancers approached him, and he quickly shooed them away. Once he had his beer he turned and stood, taking in the room. I frowned, wondering what he was up to. Then his eyes locked with mine across the room and he started towards me. I muttered a curse. When he stopped in front of the table I said, "Was that a fucking invitation?"

The young man smiled at me. "Is that any way to greet an officer, Sergeant?"

"You ain't no fucking officer," I shot back at him.

"Shows, does it?"

"You stick out like dog's balls," Marty grunted.

"Mind if I sit down?" the man asked.

I was curious and said, "Sure, why not?"

He sat and said, "You Sergeant John Kane?"

"Maybe."

"The one they call the Reaper?"

I was starting to feel nervous. Months in the jungle had taught me to be wary, and my eyes darted around the room looking for concealed enemies. "Who the fuck are you, mister?"

"Calvin Stuart."

"Is that your right name?"

"It'll do for now," he replied.

"What do you want with me?"

He looked around the room. "Is there somewhere we can go and talk?"

Satisfied that he wasn't going to try and kill me, I nodded. "Sure."

I climbed from my seat and took the beer with me. I led him out the back room where all the cribs were. It was like some kind of feral zoo with loud grunts and false cries of ecstasy flooding the room.

I pulled back a curtain and was greeted by the sight of a stark white ass rising and falling, the legs of the woman he was rutting with wrapped around his waist. In the corner sat another dancer masturbating as she watched. I shook my head and walked along until I found a vacant crib. Holding the curtain aside I said, "In here."

Pulling the curtain back across, I said, "Talk, you're interrupting my R&R."

"You haven't got a better place?"

"You think any one in here is going to give a shit about two guys talking? They're too busy screwing their brains out or jacking off while someone else does."

Stuart nodded. "All right. I was told you and your team are pretty good at what you do."

"We get by," I replied.

"I need you to go back out into the field for me and look at a village just across the border in Cambodia."

I stared at him for a while. It wasn't like he was asking me to do something I haven't done before but still there had to be a reason. "Why?"

"I can't tell you that."

With a shake of my head, I gave a derisive snort. "Fuck you, pal."

"Just wait," he blurted out as I turned to leave.

"All I can tell you is that the mission is important, and we need to know what you find there."

"By 'we' you mean the CIA, right?"

"Yes."

"What is this village we're meant to look at?"

"It's supposed to be abandoned."

I nodded. "And is it, Stuart?"

"We're not sure. That's what we want you and your team to find out."

"We've only just started R&R," I pointed out not sure if I wanted to do another mission across the fence.

"I can give you a couple of days if you want, after that I'll expect you to be at CCS." CCS was Command and Control South. "I'll meet you there to brief you."

"What about?" I asked. "You'll tell me fuck all as you've already done."

"Will you do it?" Stuart asked, ignoring my gripe.

I shrugged. "All right, we'll do it."

"Thank you, I'll see you then."

"Uh, huh." I grunted. Then, "Billy?"

"Yeah, Reaper?" came the reply from one of the cribs.

"We're going out in two days. Make the most of it."

"Aw, Fuck."

I smiled. "Two days, Billy."

"Copy that."

***

When I returned to the table, I found Marty and Jack still there. The thing was, there was a dark haired, dark eyed marine captain with a thin scar on his right cheek, there with them. "Well, ain't this the day for it," I growled.

He looked at me, studied my tired face, then, "What was that?"

"What do you want?"

"Is that any way to talk to an officer, soldier?" he demanded.

This guy was an officer. The real deal not like CIA Stuart. Still there was something about this guy that rubbed me the wrong way. "Sorry. What the fuck do you want, *sir*?"

"You SF guys think you're something special?" he snapped. "I'm here to tell you that you're not. Also to give you a warning. Don't go to Tiền đồn."

Marty suddenly straightened up. His eyes narrowed and he growled, "Who the hell are you, mister?"

"Someone who has more pull than you, soldier."

"The hell you say. Can you run, sunshine?"

Suddenly I was worried. "Marty."

"What?" the captain asked.

Marty's hand appeared from below the table with his handgun in it. He slammed it down on the table and said, "If you can run, sunshine, I'd start right now because I've had enough of your shit—"

"Marty, stop."

"—and I'm going to shoot you in the ass."

Suddenly I was suspicious. The captain didn't move but four guys appeared and set up a perimeter where we were sitting. I studied each of them, big, mean, armed. I reached out and grabbed Marty's arm. "Just relax, buddy. Just relax."

He took his hand away from the gun and placed it in his lap.

"Wise move, Sergeant," the captain said.

"Who are you?" I asked.

"Someone you'd do well not to piss off, son. Just do as I say and stay the hell away from Tiền đồn. Understood?"

I nodded slowly. "Yeah, I understand."

The marine captain stood up. "Good. Enjoy your leave, boys."

I watched him nod to his men and they fell in behind him and walked away. My eyes followed them to the door when another man caught my attention. This guy wasn't a soldier. He was CIA. Things had just gotten very interesting indeed.

"You should have let me put one in his ass, Reaper," Marty growled.

"Then his goons would have killed you, Marty. And I'd be out the best One-One in SOG."

"They'd have tried. Who the fuck was he anyway?"

"You're missing the bigger question, Marty. How did he know we were SF?"

I took Marty's handgun from the table and tucked it into my waistband. Then I nudged his beer towards him. "Have a drink and forget about it."

He grabbed the bottle. "Yeah, fuck it."

**

The Huey lifted from the muddy ground, heading skywards. As I watched it, I could see the soldier sitting in the door next to the gunner. His face was painted black, and I knew he was part of a team going out. No sooner was it airborne when I saw it joined by another Huey and two gunships. I wondered where they were going and whether they would return.

"ST Sitka," a voice said from beside me breaking into my thoughts. "Dick Reynolds One-Zero."

I turned and saw Stuart standing there in greens. "I know Dick. Where are they going?"

"There's a report of an NVA camp five klicks over the fence in Bravo Three. They're going to have a look."

I grunted and silently wished them luck.

"Welcome to Command-and-Control South, Buôn Ma Thuột," Stuart said. "Where are the rest of your men?"

"They're around here somewhere. I left them while I came looking for you."

"Round them up and meet me at the briefing tent," he said before turning and walking away.

When I found them, they were drinking beer at a tent. Why wouldn't they be, they were about to go out on another mission and possibly not come back. "Didn't take you long, did it?"

Billy looked at me with a sheepish grin. "Just enjoying a quiet one, Reaper."

"Yeah, well, we've got a briefing. Get your shit together."

Apart from my three guys, I'd also brought Jimmy and Scotty with us. Audie was still not fit enough to go on this mission.

We went over to the briefing tent and found Stuart there waiting for us. There was no one else. "Good, you're here. Gather around this table."

The map covered only a portion of Cambodia, the part where we were to operate. Stuart said, "Gentlemen, what we need from you is to insert into Cambodia and recon this village here close to the border." He pointed a long, slender index finger to a small dot.

I looked down and studied the map for a moment. It was about twenty klicks from our last insert. "What's it called?"

"Tiên đồn."

There it was. "What are we doing there?"

"Just a recon mission. Insert, have a look around, observe for a couple of days and then come home."

I looked at my men skeptically. "That's it?"

"That's it."

I leaned forward. "All right, shit for brains, how about you tell us what the hell is really going on?"

"I—I don't understand."

"After you came to us the other day, we were approached by some marine captain who told us in no uncertain terms to stay away from Tiên đồn. When—"

"Wait, when was this?" Stuart asked.

"Just after you left."

"Shit. Was there anyone else with him?"

"Yeah, a CIA spook."

"Are you sure?"

"I'm sure."

"What did he look like?"

I shook my head. "I couldn't really tell."

There was something troubling Stuart. "Who is he?"

"It doesn't matter. I still need you to go in and recon that village."

"Listen, Stuart, these guys knew we were SF."

"I can't worry about that now. Like I said, I still need you to go. If not, I'll have to replace Denver with another team."

Typical CIA bullshit, I thought to myself. "What's the alternative?"

"You can report to Command and Control North. I hear tell they're looking for teams to go into the Prairie Fire OA."

"Fuck that, Reaper," Marty said to me. "Let's take the short jump."

I still didn't like it but I shrugged. "All right. How many teams are in the area?"

"None, it's been kept clear. In fact, we're running a mission ten klicks north with ST Houston. They'll go in an hour before you do. The plan is for them to make themselves known to draw troops in the area towards them."

"Insertion?"

"King Bee helicopter."

"I want to take a ride out there this afternoon and look over possible LZs," I told him.

Stuart stared at me and said, "Not going to happen."

"You want me to insert with my team, we do this the right way."

"Fine."

"Good, get me a pilot and an Oscar Deuce. We'll go within the hour."

***

The jungle below was thick triple canopy, lush and green, with faint traces of steam wafting up through the trees. The Cessna flew a lazy eight high up so I could make out any possible LZs and mark them on my map. From there we went on to mark another two, so we had a primary, secondary, and alternate. Three LZs might seem like overkill but it wouldn't be the first time that a team had been shot out of two LZs and been forced to use the third. I looked at the pilot, Tank Yates and said into my mic, "Head north. Find another couple possible LZs. Circle them a little lower. We'll give Charlie something to think about."

He nodded and turned the Cessna so that it was pointed in the right direction.

Five miles to the north of the target area we found another open area big enough for a King Bee to touch down. The pilot dropped lower, and we flew over the clearing, only to begin taking small arms fire from the verdant landscape surrounding it.

"Shit, Reaper, you figure that they're expecting something down there?" Yates said as he maneuvered the Skymaster away from the buzzing rounds.

"Glad I'm not going in there tomorrow," I said as the bullet strikes on the plane ceased. I took my pencil and marked it on the map. "Find one more."

"Roger that."

This time we flew to the northwest until we found a suitable LZ. Yates performed the same low flyover as he had over the last dummy LZ, only this time we took no ground fire. He pulled the nose of the Cessna up and we climbed towards the clear blue sky once more.

"Covey! Covey! Covey! This is Papa One-Zero, over." There was a break in transmission and then, "Covey! Covey! Covey! This is Papa One-Zero, do you read? Over."

I could hear the gunfire in the background of the raised voice. Right away I knew there was a team in trouble and their One-Zero was radioing for help. I also knew that the Papa callsign was Dick Reynolds's ST Sitka.

"Why isn't Covey answering?" I asked Yates.

"Could be any number of reasons, but you're right. He should be on channel."

"Covey! Covey! Covey! This is Papa One-Zero, over."

I'd heard enough. "Papa One-Zero this is Snake Eater Six-Four on Channel, over."

"Good...voice...Eater..."

"Say again, Papa One-Zero, over." I looked at Yates. "Head east."

Yates put the plane into a turn. "Papa One-Zero this is Snake Eater Six-Four, over."

"Snake Eater Six-Four, this is Papa One-Zero, we're under heavy enemy fire. I say again, heavy enemy fire. We need immediate air support and assistance, over."

That was better. "Roger, Papa. Give me your coordinates, over." I looked at Yates again. "Where the fuck is their covey?"

"Beats me, Reaperman."

Reynolds gave me his coordinates and I radioed for air support. I was assured there would be a brace of helicopter gunships onsite within twenty minutes. "Papa One-Zero, copy?"

"We're still here, Snake Eater, over."

I could hear the gunfire in the background, and it sounded as though it was growing in intensity.

"Gunships will be onsite in about twenty mikes. Keep your head down."

"Charlie is getting mighty friendly down here, Reaper. Not sure will be able to hold for twenty," he replied using my name in the clear. "Ammo's getting down too."

"What's your status?"

"Two wounded, one KIA."

"All right, Dick. We'll be over your position in a few mikes. Good luck."

I turned to Yates. "Get us over them, Tank."

"What are you going to do? Throw rocks at them?" he asked me, already having an idea.

I reached down for my CAR-15 and the spare ammo which I carried. I'd flown covey a few times; it was a job that One-Zeros did for their comrades on the ground because if you were neck deep in shit, it always felt better to have someone overhead who'd been in the same situation. "We're going to help them stay alive."

***

Ten minutes later, and I knew everything I needed to. Smoke billowed from numerous explosion sites, and I could assume that the NVA were now using mortars on the men on the ground. I could also see the muzzle flashes from the long grass where the SOG men were staked out in their wagon wheel perimeter.

All around them were other flashes winking like sun catching diamonds. These men were in serious trouble. I grabbed the radio handset and said in a clear voice, "This is Snake Eater Six-Four calling any fast movers on channel, over."

At first there was nothing then a voice crackled in the receiver. "Snake-Eater Six-Four this is Weasel One-One, reading you on channel, over."

I felt relief at hearing the voice coming back to me. Weasel One-One was the commander of a flight of two Super Sabres which were loaded with napalm. I told him of ST Sitka's predicament, and he told me he was five mikes out. That would put him on arrival about the same time as the gunships.

I turned to Yates and said over the comms, "Take us down there, Tank."

"Roger that."

"Papa, this is Snake Eater. Pop smoke, I say again, pop smoke."

"Roger, Snake Eater, popping smoke."

A few moments later I saw green smoke rise from the grass. "I see green smoke, Dick."

"That's us, Reaperman."

"Keep your heads down, we're coming in on a north-south run."

"Make it quick, these guys are just about on top of us."

As the Skymaster came in at treetop level I opened the door as best I could and fired my CAR-15 at the flashes that I saw. It was almost pitiful, but it was what we had and just like that, it was over.

"Get us back around," I said to Yates.

He put the plane in a tight turn, and we repeated the run. This time however we could both hear the bullet strikes on the fuselage of the plane. Yates pulled back on the yoke and brought the nose up. As we climbed out of the fire zone, the fast air arrived. I listened intently as Dick Reynolds called in the jets giving them coordinates and directions. Soon the area was alive with rolling orange and black as the napalm dispersed on impact. From where I sat, the wall of fire looked a magnificent sight.

Hot on the heels of the first one's departure, the second came in following the directions that the One-Zero on the ground gave it. Based on my past experience, I know that to those on the ground the action seems like it takes hours but from where I sat above, it was only a matter of minutes.

Once the jets had expended their loads the gunships came in. As I watched them, I could see a King Bee trailing along behind. Good, that was the extract chopper.

For the next few minutes, the gunships expended all their heavy ordnance and most of their machine gun ammunition. Then came the call for the King Bee. It flew in, and having been in that situation many times, I knew it was taking fire. But those South Vietnamese pilots had some big balls on them, and they never flinched.

I saw every last man loaded in. Including wounded and dead. Then the helicopter lifted skyward, and ST Sitka was on its way home.

***

We were kitted up and ready to go, the hot extract of ST Sitka from the day before still fresh in my mind. Even as I watched Houston take to the air with gunship escort. Their One-Zero was a Texan by the name of Cliff Franks. Like me he was a sergeant who'd been running his own team for a while now. I saw him give me a salute as he took off and I returned it almost robotically.

I sensed movement beside me and turned to see

Stuart there. "You ready to go?"

"Yeah. We're good. Any changes?"

"There could be some weather moving in while you're on target," he explained to me. "It could get tricky if you guys get caught up with the NVA."

"We're used to it. Extra ammo, claymores, we'll be fine."

"I've assigned Tank Yates as your covey pilot. Dick Reynolds will fly in the seat beside him."

I was surprised and my face must have shown it. Stuart said, "He insisted when he heard you were going out. I guess he figures he owes you one."

"Where is he?"

"I'd say he's getting ready to take off. As you should be."

I nodded and went to find my team—

—who were waiting for me. Billy checking his shotgun for the twentieth time and Jack his M-79. "You all good to go?"

"Roger that."

I looked at our two Yards. Both were as calm as ever. "Jimmy? Scotty?"

"Good, Boss."

"Marty? Radio?"

"Good to go."

I checked my CAR-15 and satisfied, I nodded. "ST Denver, mount up."

***

The insert went according to plan. I held my team on the LZ until the King Bee had lifted off and then we headed into the triple canopy jungle. Once we were inside, I held the team up momentarily. I sent Jimmy and Scotty to scout the trail ahead while I contacted

Covey. Once contact was secured, we then rose to our feet and began our torturous walk through the undergrowth.

After two hours of slow moving, I called a halt. Scotty was on point while Billy walked safety at the rear. Marty moved up beside me and we consulted the map. I put my grimy finger on it and said, "This is where we are. The camp should be about here. Maybe another hour."

Marty nodded. "We should circle around to the high ground here where we can get a look into the village. It'll be a good defensive area if we need it. Also, down the other side of the ridge looks to be open land where we could get evaced if we need it."

I looked at him and said in a low voice, "Why is it you don't run your own team?"

"Because you'd have no one to save your sorry ass every time it gets into trouble." He shook his head and gave me a smirk.

He was right. Even though he would make a great One-Zero, he was an even better One-One. I grinned, showing my white teeth against the dark face-painted back drop. "Get your One-One ass on point."

His grin was as wide as mine. "Yes, sir."

We started moving again, Marty taking us on a circuitous route to the base of a high ridge. We climbed up it through the jungle making our regular slow progress. We were halfway up when the rain came. Leaden clouds closed in and then dumped their usual bucket loads of water upon us. The slope became slippery as torrents of water flowed down it, turning already damp earth into mud.

It took us an extra hour to reach a good site where

we could observe the village. By then the weather had really closed in and it would soon be night. So, I reached out to Covey and told them we were good for the night, and we would see them in the morning.

Just before dark, the rain stopped, and we managed to get a look at the village. It appeared quiet, deserted. I said to Marty, "What do you think?"

"It's quiet."

"Yeah."

"Maybe someone could go down and have a look while it's dark," he suggested quietly.

I nodded. "Possible. But you know the NVA. They come out when the sun goes down."

Marty gave me a pained look.

"What?"

"Do you really think that the CIA are looking for NVA down there?"

The man was thinking the same as me. "No, not after what's happened since the spook came to us."

"Well?"

"I'll take Jimmy down there with me after it gets dark. You set up a defensive perimeter here. Put all of the claymores out."

"Roger that."

"We need to know what this is all about," I said to him. "Something isn't right, and it gives me a bad feeling."

***

Jimmy and I reached the edge of the village around midnight after slipping through our perimeter and navigating the slope down to the base of the ridge. When we reached the foot of the slope, we found a narrow creek swollen with the waters washing down from the mountains upstream. We waded across, keeping our weapons above water height, and then stopped at the edge of the village.

It was dark, but the clouds had cleared enough to let some moonlight through. Failing that, I had a small flashlight which I could use should the need arise. I dropped to my knee and whispered to Jimmy, "Let's take a look around."

Slipping into the village, we worked our way through the shadows, going from hut to hut but finding nothing.

Once we were done, I said to Jimmy. "Time to go. There's nothing here."

He opened his mouth to say something when I heard two explosions. I spun around to see the ridge lighting up where the rest of my team was hiding.

"Fuck," I hissed and dropped to a knee in the middle of the village. As I stared at the ridgeline more explosions happened. But amongst it, before each blast, I could hear the deep-throated whomp of the mortar rounds kicking off.

This was bad. Not only did they have mortars but the cacophony of small arms fire was growing in intensity. I tapped Jimmy and said, "Come on."

We ran towards the creek, wading across it and started up the slope. I'd not gone far when Jimmy grabbed me. "Boss. No good."

I turned. "What?"

"No good, boss. Too many VC."

I listened for a moment. He was right. There was no way we would get through to the defensive position that Marty and the others had set up. "Shit!"

"Come, this way," he said and began moving away from the fighting along the base of the ridge.

"Where the fuck are you going?" I hissed at him.

"We go this way, then up. Come around behind."

What he said made sense, so I started to follow him. I just hoped that the others could hang on.

For the next hour we pushed hard up the ridge, all the while hearing the firing dwindle until it ceased altogether. Although I hoped, I knew deep down that it wasn't a good sign. Maybe they had broken contact and slipped into the thick jungle. Maybe.

The higher we climbed, the harder the going became until we crested. I stopped Jimmy and said, "We go this way, along the ridge."

"OK, Boss," was all he said and started walking.

Thirty minutes later, we heard voices. Vietnamese voices—and an American. The situation was indeed all fucked up.

***

Jimmy and I went to ground for the rest of the night until daylight. We had no radio, and the only thing I had apart from ammunition and grenades was two smoke cannisters—one green and the other red—plus my signaling mirror. I gently shook Jimmy awake and said into his ear. "Time to move."

At the words, the young Yard was wide awake. He sat up and said, "I go."

"No," I said assertively with a shake of my head. "We both go."

"Better me," he insisted.

I thought about it. As a team we were good at moving through the jungle, but this was his domain.

"All right. Be careful."

Jimmy rose to his feet and slipped into the jungle like a sleek cat. While he was gone, I contemplated the voices we'd heard in the dark hours. I just couldn't shake the sound of the American voice, but what the hell was going on?

Thirty minutes later, he was back. I could see the nervous look on his face. "Gone," he said. "All gone."

"What do you mean all gone?"

"No one left. All dead."

My blood ran cold. "Show me."

He led the way to the site where we'd left the team the night before. It looked like a war zone. Craters from mortars, spent shell casings, and the jungle had been stripped. But there were no bodies, only copious amounts of blood. I spent ten minutes looking around, trying to find someone, anyone. When it dawned on me that I was going to find no one, my mood turned dark. Then a sudden thought permeated my brain. How the hell was I going to get Jimmy and me out of there?

***

There was only one way to go, and that was towards the border. We had water, ammunition, and some food. If we needed to, we could live off the jungle. We started out slowly, trying not to trigger anything that would tip off the enemy that there were still men there alive.

Enemy? I had no idea who the enemy even was. Just after midday I thought I heard a plane. I ordered Jimmy to halt while we remained silent in the jungle and listened. If it was a plane, it was gone because I never heard it again for the rest of the day.

It wouldn't take long for us to be officially posted as missing.

That night we hunkered down in a thick patch of undergrowth. The bugs were thicker than flies around a dead carcass, but you get used to them after a while.

The following morning, we continued on.

It was around noon when I heard the plane again. This time it was getting closer. I reached for my mirror and then turned to Jimmy. "We need to get somewhere a bit clearer. So they can see us."

We pushed harder, fully aware that we could be informing anyone within ear shot of our position. Ahead of us the jungle opened up into a large clearing covered with elephant grass. Both Jimmy and I waited there, listening. The last thing we wanted to do was miss an opportunity, but to rush headlong out into it where an NVA force could be hiding was just stupid.

Using hand signals, I told Jimmy to look around while I listened to the drone of the plane. It was somewhere off to the east and steadily coming closer. The sound of the plane faded but then grew louder again. I figured whoever it was, was possibly flying a search pattern or—it suddenly dawned on me. If ST Denver was listed as missing, then maybe a Brightlight team had been inserted. A Brightlight team came into the AO to help extract teams that were in trouble if needed, or to bring out bodies. They would also recover downed pilots or lost or wounded operators. Brightlights were dangerous. Most of the time Charlie was waiting for them. The men on these teams were often the toughest and most experienced hitters SOG had. If there was a team, then the plane could be flying covey for them.

Then my heart fell for a moment. No, there would be no Brightlight team. We had been working for the CIA. We were probably already written off. One glimmer of hope, if I knew my comrades, they wouldn't let it go at that. Maybe, just maybe, Dick Reynolds had pulled something together off his own bat.

So, I waited and listened clutching onto my CAR-15 just in case.

The plane's engine came and went and after twenty minutes, I heard the faint displacement of vegetation to my front. I brought the CAR-15 up slowly and slid my finger through the trigger guard. Then Jimmy emerged; just materialized in front of me.

"How's it look?" I asked him in a hushed voice.

"Good. No VC."

I nodded and looked back up at the sky. Clouds were gathering on the horizon and soon a storm would be rolling in. And that plane wasn't getting any closer. I looked at Jimmy and pointed in the direction the sound of the plane came from. "What do you think?"

"Brightlight."

I nodded. "Could be. Let's go."

Jimmy led the way, back in the opposite direction towards the abandoned village. If we were right, then all well and good. We had hope. If we were wrong, we were just as screwed as before.

Our big problem was time. If there was a Brightlight team on the ground then they would possibly stay out one night, max. If they made contact, they'd pull out even sooner. It was quite common for a Brightlight team to take casualties, as was the nature of the beast. It was mostly expected, but they still went anyway.

ST Denver had been on two. Both times we'd taken heavy fire and been shot out of the AO. We were one and two for recovery. All of us had sustained some kind of wound. Now there was only two of us left.

We walked all night, resting every couple of hours. From the time the sun came up we relied on hand signals for communication just in case there were any NVA close. It had something to do with the footprints we'd seen not long after dawn.

It was around eleven hundred when I heard the plane again. We halted in a thinner patch of jungle, and I listened once more. This time the plane drew closer. Kept coming on.

Hurriedly I looked around. "We need to get clearer," I told Jimmy.

A few minutes later we found an opening in the canopy which allowed sunlight to shine down. I took out the mirror I carried and once again we waited.

This time, however, the plane kept coming. I started using the mirror, reflecting the sunlight upward, hoping against all hope to catch the eye of whoever was on board.

The plane was a Bird Dog. It flew low and right over the top of us giving no indication it had seen my signals. It flew on and I felt my heart sink. Then it turned. Not just a normal, lazy turn, but a sharp, tight turn which put it back on course to fly over our location.

They'd seen us. I worked the mirror again and this time the pilot waggled his wings as he passed over. It was a crazy thing to do. Such an act, if seen by the enemy, would inform them of our location, but knowing we had radio troubles, it was a way of letting us know we were seen, and help was coming.

I looked at Jimmy. "We'll do a sweep and meet back here. If something happens, we meet at that creek we crossed a way back."

Jimmy nodded and melted into the undergrowth.

***

The Brightlight team was ST Waco. They were led by One-Zero, Chuck Wallis. He was an SF sergeant out of Amarillo, Texas. His One-One was a fresh-faced kid from New York. Henry Best. The rest of their team were Yards.

Like Jimmy had earlier, they just materialized out of the jungle. One moment there was nothing, the next they were there. Wallis approached me. We'd met over beers a few times before he was transferred north to CCN. He crouched beside me and said in a low voice, "What the hell are you up to, Reaper?"

"I'll tell you about it when we get back."

"Where are the rest of your team?"

"Gone."

"Shit. You sure?"

"As sure as I can be."

He shook his head and spat into the damp earth at his feet. "Damnit. Maybe they'll put a Hatchet force in to see what they can find."

"They won't find nothing. We didn't."

Wallis waved his One-One over. "Henry, get Covey on the horn. Tell them we've found two survivors from Denver and we're making for the secondary LZ."

I looked at him and Wallis shrugged. "Charlie isn't far behind us. Maybe company size. We need to go now."

"Who is Covey?"

"Tank and Reynolds. Dick wasn't about to leave you out here. He was the one who insisted on a Brightlight mission. Crawled so far up the commander's ass that he had no choice but to say yes if he wanted to get rid of him."

I smiled. That's the type of comradery we had in the Recon teams. I'd known one man to get off a chopper and search the jungle for a missing team when it was thought suicidal. He'd been told it was crazy, he was a fool, but he went anyway. In the end, after four hours on the ground, he brought out a wounded survivor. The crazy son of a bitch who'd done it, was Dick Reynolds.

"Remind me to buy him a beer."

"You can buy me one too. Let's go."

I nodded, wishing I knew the exact fate of the rest of my men. "Lead the way, Chuck."

THE PRESENT...

Kane looked up from the diary. Stuart was dozing on the sofa. He looked back down at the diary and tried to process the part that he'd read. He knew his grandfather had fought in Vietnam, even been a Recon man. That was part of—no, the whole reason he'd become one himself. But he hadn't known his grandfather had served with SOG. Not that he'd talked about it much.

"Something the matter, son?" Stuart asked, coming out of his nap. "You might be a fast reader but not even you could read it all in that time."

"What happened to his men?" Kane asked.

"What it says in there. They were missing. Their names on the wall have MIA next to them. Hell, everyone knows they're dead."

"What happened to them?"

"Let him tell you in his own words."

Kane still wasn't satisfied. "Why him? Why did you pick him?"

Stuart turned his head to look at Kane. "Because he was good."

"Weren't there other teams you could have picked for the mission?"

"Sure, but I chose him."

"Again, why?"

"Because he was a stubborn son of a bitch who didn't know when to let up," Stuart growled. "Looks like you inherited some of his qualities."

"It says in the diary that he heard American voices and that he was warned off it by an American CIA officer. Who were they?"

Stuart sighed, pulling himself into a sitting position on the edge of the sofa. "Bad men."

"That's it?"

"Son, you've been in battle. What happens to the plan after the first shot is fired."

"Don't try that shit on me, old man. I'm—"

"What happens?" Stuart snapped.

"It goes to shit."

"Got it in one. Everything went to shit."

"How?" Kane was like a dog with a bone.

The former CIA officer lay back down, rolling over, presenting his back to Kane. "Read the fucking diary."

SOUTH VIETNAM, 1968...

I slammed him so hard against the side of the Huey that I saw the bastard's teeth rattle in his head. "They're dead, you son of a bitch. My whole team except for us. Fucking gone."

Before I knew it, my sidearm was out and pressed against the side of Stuart's head in my trembling fist. "This is all fucked up. Maybe you should fucking join them."

I felt strong hands grab me as Wallis and his One-One hauled me away from the CIA man. The Waco commander disarmed me and shoved me backward. "Cool off, Reaper. Now is not the time. Go get cleaned up, see the boss, then come find me."

I did as he suggested. Had a shower, got cleaned up, and then went looking for my commanding officer. However, it was Stuart who found me first. "I need to debrief you."

"Yeah? Well I need to see my commanding officer and explain to him how I lost my fucking team."

I stormed off but he followed me to the command bunker. I thought about shooting him but didn't. Once inside I saw the colonel. Greg Roberts was in his late thirties, his hair so short it was almost shaved. Stuart followed me in.

"Good to have you back, Kane," he said to me. "We just about had you written off."

"Not hardly, sir."

"Just waiting for the G-2 officer then we'll get started."

"What happened out there, Kane?" Stuart wasn't about to wait. "What did you find?"

I turned and stared at him. "How about you tell me."

"Damn it, Kane, this was my mission."

"Just hold up, Stuart. We wait for the G-2 officer and then we go through it."

The intelligence officer arrived a couple of minutes later. Once he was ready with a map on the table in front of us, Roberts said, "All right, son, start at the beginning."

"The insert was fine, no problems. We moved on the target in the AO and set up an OP on the ridge here. It gave us a good view of the village below."

"Was there anyone there?" Stuart asked me.

I looked at the colonel who nodded. "We couldn't see anyone, so I decided to take one of our Yards down for a look."

"And?"

"It was deserted. No one there. We had just started back when the rest of the team on the ridge were attacked."

"By who?" the colonel asked.

"I don't know—I mean I kind of do but it didn't seem right."

I could see Stuart staring at me, his burning gaze not moving. "Who were they?" I asked him in a not too friendly tone.

"I don't know. I wasn't there."

"The fuck you don't," I growled.

"Continue, Sergeant," the G-2 officer said.

"Jimmy and I worked our way around them. When we were almost there we stopped. That was when we heard the American voices."

"What American voices?" the colonel asked. "Your team?"

"No." I turned my gaze on Stuart again. "Who the fuck were they? You know who they were, you son of a bitch. I know you do."

"Are you sure they were American?" Stuart asked me.

"I'm certain," I replied. "You still haven't answered my question."

Once again, he ignored it.

"I'm sorry about your team," he said, before looking at the colonel. "Even so, I'd consider the mission a success. I have what I need."

My voice was bitter. "I'm glad you got whatever it is you fucking needed. Good men paid for it in blood."

"It's not like that."

"Then how is it?"

"We needed to know what was going on in that village. Now we know."

"We'll send a Hatchet force—"

"No," Stuart said adamantly. "A B-52 strike will be ordered and the area carpet bombed."

"What if my men are still alive?" I asked stupidly.

"They won't be."

I knew he was right. It was just a desperate, helpless thing to say.

I turned away and stared at the wall of the bunker. Behind me the colonel said, "I guess that's it. My first instinct is to put you in command of a new team, John, and send you back out into another AO. But something is telling me you need some time. Take a few days. Get drunk and blow off some steam. All right?"

I turned and nodded. "Yes, sir."

"Good."

"One more thing," Stuart said to me before I could leave the command center. "You don't mention a word of this to anyone."

Staring at him, my eyes burned with fire. "Fuck you."

***

Mama San's was busy as usual. But I wasn't there for the beer or ass. My mission was to gain intel. If the CIA wasn't going to tell me why my friends died, then I'd find out for myself. First, I started asking around about a Marine captain with dark hair, broad build, thin scar on his right cheek.

I started with the girls, but every GI looked the same to them. Then I went to the soldiers; maybe they knew something. One of them, a sergeant from Newark looked at me as though I was crazy. "Man, there's not been a Marine around here for a month or so."

Suddenly I knew he was right. I don't know why I didn't think it was odd when the son of a bitch showed up just after Stuart. Maybe he was CIA after all. I could have sworn he wasn't, but...

"How about CIA?" I asked him.

He shook his head. "Nope, nothing. Mind you, it don't mean they weren't here. You might try the Black Dragon down the street. You might get luckier there."

I nodded. The Black Dragon was a joint frequented by officers. It wasn't more upmarket, just a place they hung out without being around enlisted men. I was about to leave when one of the working girls came over to me. Her hair was down her back, around her eyes was a thick layer of makeup, and her small nipples stuck out of her breasts like thimbles. "You want suck, Joe? Make you relax, have a beer while I do."

I shook my head. The last thing I felt like was some mama swinging off my dick. "No, I'm fine."

Once again, I tried to leave but she grabbed my arm. My anger flared but as I glared at her I could see something in her eyes. She said, "Maybe you want fuck instead? I very good, very horny. You come with me."

I nodded slowly. "All right."

She took my hand and led me through the tables and out into a back room. Once inside she looked up at me. "You look for man?"

Taken aback, I said, "What do you mean?"

"You look for man, you ask questions."

"Yes. He was dressed as a marine."

"Him come few nights back. Him flyer."

I was confused. "Flyer?"

She nodded vigorously. "Yes. Him pilot."

I described the man again. "You're sure it was him?"

"That him. He want fuck. Get rough."

She tilted her head up and showed me the already fading bruises on her throat.

"He did that?" I asked.

"Uh, huh."

"Why are you telling me this?"

"Maybe you kill him."

"I can't kill him if I can't find him."

"I know where he is," she said to me. "Him at Dragon."

"The Black Dragon?"

She nodded. "Yes."

"How do you know?"

"I have friend there. She tell me."

I looked at her for a moment, trying to figure out if she was telling the truth or not. I decided that she was. "Thank you. I'll go and check it out."

She stepped back. "You sure you no want before go?"

I smiled at her. "Maybe next time."

***

The Black Dragon was not as busy as Mama San's had been. It cost me money at the front door to get in, but I wasn't worried. The place was red from the lights and the bar room was filled with smoke. The scent of hooch was thick, and I got a few crooked stares from some of the officers.

It wasn't the first time I'd been in here. The other time I'd been asked to leave by a colonel who'd taken it upon himself to point out that the Black Dragon was officers only. I just hoped I found out something before it happened again. And from the look I was getting from an Airborne captain who was getting his knob polished by a skinny-assed prostitute, I knew it wouldn't be far away. Unless she was any good at what she did and distracted him a little bit longer.

I took a pull on my beer and swilled it around in my mouth before I swallowed. It was a habit I picked up when I was running missions. I placed it back on the scarred tabletop on the wet ring where it had been before.

Two lieutenants made a noise as they entered and were met near the front door by two eager working girls wearing only panties.

Once more my eyes scanned the room as I looked for my target. Still nothing. I didn't have long to wait, however, because they came to me. And when I say 'they', I mean the guy I was looking for and his CIA friend. Both were dressed in fatigues and wearing all the right adornments for the Air Cav.

I tensed as they sat down.

"Well, well," the man I knew as a Marine captain said as he sat down. "Short a few friends I see."

Right at that time I wanted nothing more than to shoot him in that smug face of his. However, I'd noticed three other men looking our way. All were South Vietnamese. So, I just stared at him.

"Cat got your tongue?"

I shifted my gaze to his friend. My right hand resting on the butt of my sidearm. "You were warned," he said.

"So, what is it you're doing out there?" I asked them.

"It's a secret."

I nodded. "Who are your friends?"

"What friends?"

"The three ARVNs you brought with you. They're the only reason you two assholes are still alive."

"Talks tough, don't he?"

"I kill tougher."

"Maybe we'll find out."

"You'd better hurry because I'm coming after you and I'm not going to stop until you're all in the ground."

"That would be a mistake."

"If it is, you made it. Now, piss off before I start shooting anyway."

They stood up. "This isn't over."

"Bring it on."

I watched them go, my hands trembling with adrenalin at the confrontation and anger at their audacity to not deny their actions. I took a pull of my beer and then sat there staring at it. "Fuck it," I said and got to my feet.

The night was as humid as shit outside and almost felt like I was back in the jungle. I touched the weapon at my side as I glanced around looking to see if there was any indication as to the way they had gone.

"Once again, John, a day late and a dollar short."

I turned and went back inside, breasting the bar and buying another beer. I'd just turned away when three Asian men dressed in black pajamas, and holding AK47s, burst into the bar. My first instinct was to take cover, so I leaped over the bar just as they opened fire. Bullets hammered into the wall above where I lay, shattering bottles and glasses. More punched through the bar and the guy serving cried out as multiple rounds tore into him. Blood splattered the steadily disintegrating wall behind him.

Taking out my sidearm, I came up and fired at the first shooter I saw. Four shots, two of which missed, but not the other two. Both hit him in the chest, and he fell to the floor, losing his hold on the AK.

Around the room, more servicemen were starting to respond to the shooting as they scrambled for weapons. Some were too slow and were caught in the leaden hailstorm. Bodies started to pile up; men, prostitutes, these shooters weren't worried about who got caught up in it. I fired again and took down a second shooter. His friend's firing stopped suddenly as his magazine ran dry. He dropped the spent one out and tried to reload.

"Thôi!" I shouted. "Stop!"

He froze momentarily, his eyes staring hard at me. He screeched defiantly and tried to lift his weapon once more. This time there was no holding back as I blew off the rest of the magazine.

He jerked wildly before falling, his chest shot to hell from all the bullets I put there.

Changing out the magazine, I made sure that all threats had been neutralized before I checked them. I knelt beside the first, and closest shooter and to my surprise found that he was one of the ARVNs I had seen earlier. "What the fuck?"

"Are you all right, soldier?"

I looked up to see a captain standing over me.

He looked a little shaken but seemed to be coming good. "I'm good."

"I don't know who you are, but this could have been a lot worse if it hadn't been for you. Fucking Charlie."

I was about to inform him that these men were far from VC but clamped my mouth shut. Instead, I just nodded to him and stood up. "I'll be going now."

"The MPs will be here shortly; they'll want to talk to you."

Indicating around the room, I said, "There's plenty of witnesses."

"I don't think it's wise—"

I nodded again. "Fuck being wise."

I left the club and went outside again. Only this time I kept going. The night air stank. Trash, shit, mixed with food cooked in the open-air kitchens. I turned left and walked along the crowded street. Behind me action was happening at the club.

I weaved through the crowd. Occasionally a scantily clad prostitute emerged from a narrow laneway to proposition me, but I turned them down, not wishing to end up with an STD.

Twenty minutes later, I was walking past another club when I heard a familiar voice. "Reaper, get your ass in here."

I looked over and saw Chuck Wallis standing in the doorway of the Pink Pussy with two girls hanging off him and a beer in his hand. "What fool let you loose?"

He grinned. "You owe me a beer and a talk."

I stared at him for a moment and then glanced at

the two ladies. "Maybe next time."

"Don't worry about them, they don't even understand English."

I rolled my eyes. "All right. One beer."

***

"Holy shit," Wallis groaned and let his head fall back, his eyes closed. I waited for a moment for things to return to normal. A minute or so later the second of the two prostitutes emerged from beneath the table wiping her mouth and smiling.

I was on my third beer and halfway through the story. Wallis gathered himself and said, "So you have no idea what is going on?"

I shook my head. "All I know is that it cost me my team."

"You going back out?"

"I don't know. It won't be the same."

"I've got a place on Waco if you want it. No command responsibility."

"I'll think about it."

Wallis took a pull of his beer and sat the bottle back on the table. "You want another beer?"

The one in my hand was about empty. I was feeling kind of mellow and relaxed, all the tension from the gun fight gone out of my system. I nodded. "Yeah, get me another, besides, I'm not finished yet."

"You mean there's more?"

"Uh, huh."

"All right buddy, I'm your man, give me a moment and I'll be right back."

For the next hour I ran through everything once more, including the fight at the club. Wallis stared at me and said, "Sounds like you pissed these fuckers off, Reaper."

"You don't say."

"You need to report it," he urged me. "The next time you see them, just frag their asses before they get a chance to do anything else."

"The thought had crossed my mind."

A silence descended over us before Wallis picked up his beer and said, "ST Denver."

I followed his lead. "ST Denver."

***

I woke the next morning to a savage pounding. Not only the one in my head, but the one on the door to the room where I was sleeping. I groaned and tried to roll over but the weight across my waist stopped me. Opening my eyes, I saw the reason for it. A naked form had me pinned in place.

The banging started again. "Fuck off."

"Kane, open the door."

"What the—" My face screwed up in a frown. "Go away."

The woman lying across me stirred and her head turned towards me. It was one of the prostitutes from the night before. She opened an eye and said, "You want more?"

The pounding again.

"Christ," I muttered and dragged myself free of the petite form.

She moaned and rolled away.

I sat up on the edge of the bed and looked around through the hangover haze which fogged everything. My mouth tasted like someone shit in it and stale beer. The room I was in tripled as a bedroom, a kitchen, and a living room.

"Kane, open the door."

"Yeah, yeah. Shut up, I'm coming."

I stood up and the room spun. My senses filled with the scent of stale alcohol, and I lurched towards the sink where I emptied the contents of my stomach. "Frigging hell."

I wiped a line of drool away and staggered towards the door, collecting my sidearm as I went. When the door swung open two men stood opposite me, mouths agape. It could have been the weapon I held, but more than likely the fact that I was completely naked.

"Who are you?" I asked them.

Both men were dressed in military fatigues. "Potter and Lewis. You need to come with us."

"The fuck I do."

The door slammed in their faces, and I turned away. I muttered a few more expletives but the men outside the door weren't about to be put off. "Stuart sent us to get you."

"Tell him to fuck off." My hangover was mean, and I was quickly warming to the task.

The door crashed back, and the prostitute lurched to her feet from the bed with a yelp, her hands trying to cover her small breasts but forgetting about the dark thatch at the junction of her thighs.

I started to raise the handgun but my brain was too screwed up and my reflexes slow. The two men tackled me to the bed, disarmed me, and held me down. "Get off, you frigging assholes."

"We were told to bring you in and that's exactly what we intend to do."

"Can I at least have my pants?"

***

"What the hell do you think you're doing?" Stuart growled at me as I sat opposite him without my shirt on.

My hangover was still raw and as I glared at him, I snarled, "Looking for fucking answers."

"You were told to keep away from it."

"Maybe I'm hard of hearing," I growled back. "Or maybe if someone told me what the hell was going on we wouldn't frigging be here."

"Your work here is done. This has nothing to do with you."

"The hell it doesn't. I lost my men out there."

"I'm sorry about that but—"

"Sorry? You're sorry? Well I'm sorry that your sorry won't fucking cut it. I'm going to ride this bitch to the end, Stuart." My eyes narrowed. "I've already hit a nerve—on both sides. They came after me and they knew everything. This time I don't care if they see me coming."

Stuart stared at me and sighed. He climbed to his feet and said, "Don't go anywhere."

I sat there and waited for him to return. My only company the men inside my head hammering away and the queasy feeling in my guts. I looked around the room I was sequestered in for something to vomit in but there was nothing.

When the door opened again, I was surprised to see a general walk through. I shot to my feet. "I'd salute you, General, but my hands are kind of tied."

"Sit down, Sergeant. It seems to me we have a lot to talk about."

I sat down and waited.

The general was joined by Stuart. "This is General Hollister, Twenty-First MPs. He and I are working together. He's decided to fill you in on our operation in the hope—"

"Damn it, Stuart, cut through the crap. Kane, you're a stubborn, insubordinate, tough son of a bitch."

"Thank you—"

"Shut up, I'm not finished."

"Sir."

"It appears that you're determined to follow this all the way through whether you have permission or not. Well, fuck it. You're in now and there's no way out until it's finished. Understood?"

"Yes, sir."

"Good. Stuart."

The CIA man sighed. "I still think—"

"I didn't ask your opinion. You came to us, remember?"

I was liking this man already. Stuart said, "That AO you and your team was inserted into was believed to be part of a drug smuggling operation run by Americans and South Vietnamese collaborators."

"You're shitting me. That was why I heard American voices?"

The two men nodded. "What you heard was part of a rogue CIA team who disappeared six months ago. They were on an operation with General Tuan Pham."

"And they're operating in Cambodia? How?" I asked.

"By paying off the right people. The village you and your team hit is a way station."

"Why don't you just bomb the shit out of it or use a Hatchet Force?"

"Because before going ahead with something to that extreme, we need all the intel that can be found. They're getting it into the US, and we don't know how. That's where you come in."

"How?"

"We want you to go back out into the jungle and find out what is happening."

"When?"

"One week from today. You will have two days to pick yourself a team. After that you will disappear until you get inserted. Let the bastards think we're giving up."

I thought about it for a while before answering. "What do you want me to do, *exactly*?"

"Insert into the AO and collect any intel you can find that will help. Mission length will be four days unless you get into trouble or request an extension."

"And once it's done?"

"You get out. There will be no contact unless unavoidable. We need to know how they're getting the stuff out."

I nodded slowly. "All right. Can you get me the men I want?"

Hollister frowned at me. "Can't you?"

"The other two men I want are One-Zeros and at

the top of their game. I doubt they're going to be let go that easily."

"Give me their names," he replied wearily.

"Chuck Wallis from ST Waco and Dick Reynolds from ST Sitka. We'll take Reynolds's indigenous Yards. They're good."

"I'll have it seen to."

"Just how do you propose on keeping this a secret?" I asked them.

"You leave that to us. Right at this time, you and us are the only ones who know what's planned. Your team will join you tomorrow. You've got an hour to get ready."

"What about intel, maps, shit like that?"

Hollister stood up. "You'll get it tomorrow. Good luck, Sergeant. You're going to need it."

"One other thing, Sergeant," Stuart said to me. "I'm coming with you."

THE PRESENT...

"We have to go," Sara Harris said urgently as she strode into the room. "They've found us."

"Who has?" Kane asked, looking up as he closed the diary.

"Quan," Sara replied as she started waking Stuart up.

"Who is Quan?" Kane asked her.

"Head of the Kowloon Triad," Stuart answered for her, rubbing his face and hair.

"What's he got to do with this?" Kane asked, checking his P226.

"We don't have time for twenty questions," Roberts snapped as he appeared. "We've got seven armed men coming up here from the bottom floor. We leave now."

Kane walked over to Stuart and helped him up. "Come on, old man, let's get you out of here."

"Who the fuck you calling old man, sonny. Didn't anyone ever teach you to respect your elders? Give me a gun."

"Slow your roll, Jesse James. Just stick close to me."

They followed Roberts and Sara out into the

hallway. The lead MI6 officer turned and said, "This way."

At the end of the hallway Kane saw another man waiting for them. Roberts said, "There's a stairwell ahead."

"We can't use it," Kane said with a smirk. "The old guy won't make it."

"Damn it—"

"We're taking it down two floors. Once there we'll get the elevator to the bottom."

Kane nodded. He turned to Stuart. "Follow Sara, I'll watch our six."

Stuart chuckled. "With pleasure."

"It's the only time you can stare at my ass, Calvin," she said over her shoulder. "Remember that."

Moving quickly towards where the other agent was waiting for them, they started down the stairs. "Was a time when your grandad would have waited here and breathed fire all over these sons of bitches."

"Yeah, well, I have to find out the whole story before I do that," Kane retorted. "And to do that you need to be kept alive."

The small caravan moved slowly down two sets of stairs until they reached the landing, cautiously checking the door before entering the corridor on that floor. From there they found the elevator and rode it down to the lobby.

Roberts and the other officer who had joined them led the way through the busy foyer, with no sign of any weapons on display so as not to raise alarm amongst guests.

Halfway across the lobby, sudden gunshots rang out.

At the head of the entourage.

Kane saw Roberts and the other officer fall. Both had been shot through the torso and were dead before they hit the red marble, their blood complementing the rich color.

"Shit!" Kane hissed and shouted to Sara, "Keep moving! Get him out of here."

The man they called the Reaper looked left, noticing a shooter trying to get a clear shot through the scattering hotel guests. Kane brought his P226 up and aimed, a passage opening momentarily which he took advantage of, firing without hesitation.

The bullet flew straight and true, touching the shooter in the side of his head, snapping it sideways, and dropping him where he stood.

By now those guests who hadn't scattered were face down on the cold floor, some bleeding, others in fear of their lives. The only ones unafraid were the Kowloon Triad shooters. All five of them. There had been thirteen of them all told.

Things had just grown easier and harder at the same time.

Caught out in the open, Kane had no option but to push forward. Ahead of him he saw Sara guiding Stuart along in front of her while firing to her right at a pair of shooters, taking one down but missing the other. They made it as far as a marble column before she forced the old man behind it for cover.

Kane fired his weapon at another shooter who was armed with an automatic weapon. The first shot was hurried; missed. The shooter turned quickly and dropped to his knee, causing Kane's next round to miss as well.

"Fuck it," he growled.

The shooter opened fire and sprayed bullets in Kane's direction. There was still no cover so Kane did the only thing he could do. He dived to his left, rolled, and came up firing. Four shots, all of them hit. The shooter spilled sideways to the hard floor, losing his grip on the gun he'd been firing.

Suddenly the triad members were aware of the new threat and began taking cover. One behind a close pillar, another behind a sofa, the last leaped over the service counter.

"Sara, keep moving," Kane called out to her, aware that the shooting would bring more of the triad men from upstairs.

As she and Stuart broke cover once more, Kane spread his shots at the three positions, hoping to suppress them for just long enough. As luck would have it, the shooter behind the pillar showed too much of himself. A well-placed shot sent him staggering way from his cover. Kane fired twice more, and the shooter fell.

Cautiously moving as fast as he could, he performed a tactical reload. Once the weapon was set, he concentrated on the shooter behind the counter, firing three shots through the thin wooden veneer, forcing the hidden triad killer to his feet. As the man sprang up, Kane shot him in the head, sending bone fragments and gore splattering an inkblot pattern over the wallpaper behind. Let some psychiatrist decipher that one.

More gunshots and Kane felt the burn across his left shoulder. Turning his attention towards the origin of the shot, he saw a shooter standing behind a sofa, a panicked expression on his face as he tried to reload.

Kane said, "Shit out of luck, pal," and shot him in the head, then started running towards the main entrance where he'd seen Sara and Stuart go. Joining them again outside, he said, "We need a vehicle."

"Over there," Sara said, pointing at a dark Mercedes. "Roberts ordered it before we came down."

As they approached the valet, Kane said, "You drive. Cal, get in the back and lay down."

Sara snatched the electronic key and climbed behind the wheel while Kane shoved Stuart in the back. He slammed the door and glanced back towards the main entrance. Still inside the foyer but heading towards them were numerous armed men. He leaped into the front and said, "Time to go. Floor it."

Sara's foot went almost to the floor and the rear tires spun on the pavement damp from the night air. Navigating the oval turnaround at such a speed, the rear end slid sideways, and Sara was forced to correct it. As the Mercedes hit the street, Kane grabbed at the armrest on the door because Sara had spun the wheel hard left shifting the center of gravity.

"Where are we going?" Kane asked her.

"There is a safehouse about thirty minutes away. They know we're coming."

Then Kane thought of something else. "What about the Chinese authorities?"

"We'll have to deal with them if and when that happens."

Behind them a large SUV appeared, its lights bouncing wildly as it hit the street after jumping the curb. It was quickly followed by another, and they were soon in pursuit.

"Who the hell are these people?" Kane asked.

"Triad. They're after Cal."

"Why?"

"Not exactly sure. All I know is that Cal has information. These bastards want Cal."

Deciding to get it straight from the horse's mouth he called over his shoulder, "Why do these guys want to kill you, Cal?"

"Because I know too much." The answer was succinct.

"What about?"

"Things."

Kane shook his head. "What things?"

"Things that could put them out of business."

Kane glanced out the rear window. The SUVs were getting closer. "This isn't a game, Cal."

"Never said it was, son."

"You damn spooks are all the same."

"Exactly what your grandpa said."

"Shit."

Sara took a right ahead and then a left, knowing that she would never lose them like this, while behind them the SUVs continued to gain more ground. Soon they were close enough and started firing weapons. The bullet strikes were intermittent but eventually the rear window shattered.

"Son of a bitch," Kane growled. He raised his weapon and said, "Stay down, Cal," and commenced firing back.

Sara swerved, trying to evade their shots, but what worked for them also worked against them, hindering Kane's aim. He saw a couple of bullet strikes but nothing happened.

A couple more turns and the Mercedes finally made it to the on ramp to the three-lane highway. It was busy, like the whole place never slept. Sara weaved in and out trying to break away from their pursuers. She managed to put a good gap between them but knew it was never going to last.

"Stop the car!"

"What?" Sara's voice was high-pitched with her surprise as she risked a quick glance in Kane's direction.

"Stop the car, now."

She veered onto the shoulder and trod hard on the brake pedal, bringing the Mercedes to a shuddering stop. Kane's door flew open, and he strode purposefully towards the trunk. Standing there with his feet apart, he raised his P226 and proceeded to fire multiple rounds at the lead SUV.

Pulling suddenly in a hard right, it turned over like a misshapen barrel rolling down a hill. Behind it, the second SUV, with nowhere to go, hit it at speed. The two vehicles ripped each other apart, flinging debris across the highway. Then came a flash of orange and the first SUV burst into flames, quickly engulfing the second so both were burning fiercely, lighting the dark sky.

Kane climbed back into the Mercedes and Sara said, "That'll fuck up your evening."

"Shall we go?" Kane asked, as though he'd just finished a stroll in the park.

"Let's."

Twenty minutes later, they were at another safehouse. This one was a little less grandiose. More modest or economical you might say.

Once inside, Sara used the facilities then attempted to reach out to her bosses to keep them abreast of the night's occurrences. Meanwhile, Kane helped himself to a coffee, then sat in a chair opposite Stuart, eyeing him quizzically. "Now, where were we?"

"You were reading, and I was sleeping. Judging by the time on my watch, I still have another four or five hours until it's daylight. Now, you read the book, I'm going to sleep."

Kane watched as he got to his feet, swaying a little with the effort. Reaper lurched to his own feet to help steady the old man. "You all right?"

"I'm fine, just need some sleep is all."

"Fine, come on, let's find a sofa for you."

Once Stuart was settled, Kane sat in a reclining armchair, getting comfortable without activating the recline function—wanting to be able to react at a moment's notice—before opening the journal to where he'd been up to at the hotel. Then he started to read.

CAMBODIA, 1968...

The cloying heat of the jungle was a welcome relief. Out in front of me somewhere was Trai, one of Chuck Wallis's Yards. We'd been in the jungle for a day and were moving slowly.

When we'd all first met up at FOB 6, Wallis and Reynolds were on edge having not been informed of what was happening. Reynolds was picked out of his team, the same as Wallis and his Yards. When they saw Stuart, they knew shit was about to get real.

"What the fuck is he doing here?" Wallis had asked me in an angry hiss.

"He's coming with us," I replied.

"What do you mean, coming with us?" Wallis demanded. "Where we going, Reaper?"

"Daniel Boone AO," I replied using the codename for the Cambodian area of operations.

"The hell he is," Reynolds growled. "That's no place to bust his cherry."

"I'm going," Stuart said firmly as he joined us.

Wallis snorted. "Yeah and maybe you won't fucking come back."

Stuart took a step forward towards the rugged looking SOG man. "You fucking threatening me, asshole?"

"Maybe I am," Wallis snarled, not backing down.

I stepped between them and placed a hand on both chests, using all my strength to keep them apart. "Just calm down, both of you. You take that shit out there and we're all dead." I stared at Wallis. "You of all people should know that."

"Tell us what we're doing here. Reaper," Reynolds said, an edge to his voice.

Turning to look at him, I said, "I asked for you."

"This is you?" Wallis looked confused.

"Yes. Now, if you listen, I'll fill you in on all I know."

For the next thirty minutes I had laid it out for them, answering any questions they had. Then when I was finished, they both nodded. "We're in."

We were inserted five days later. Until then we trained and got used to each other. Before that though we were given a name. ST Albany.

The LZ was small but that was fine, the less open ground we had to cross, the better. Unlike other insertions, there was no false ones, it was in and out. However, we formed our wagon wheel and probably waited for longer than we normally would have on any other operation.

Once I was satisfied, we moved into the jungle and paused for just long enough to give the FAC (Covey) the all clear.

When we moved out, Trai was on point. I came next with Reynolds behind me carrying the radio. Following him was Stuart and then Wallis. On the tail end was the second Yard, Minh. After Stuart had been added to the team, the third Yard was left behind.

That first night I radioed in and left it at that. I repeated the call the next morning. Now we were perhaps half a day from our target and the tension levels were rising.

We stopped just after noon so we could take a break and Reynolds could give the OK signal. But when he did so he picked up some traffic.

He threw a small stick at me to gain my attention and waved me over. I crouched beside him, and he passed me the handset. "Listen."

Taking it in my right hand, I put it to my ear, hearing immediately what he meant. It was garbled and broken, but because we knew what to listen for, we could put it together. Somewhere within the range of the radio a Spike Team was in trouble.

I listened for a couple more minutes before I figured out who it was by their call sign. I looked at Reynolds and passed him the receiver. "It's Dallas."

"Shit," he whispered.

"Get in touch with Covey and see if they need help. It'll mean them going off station, but we'll manage."

"What's going on?" Wallis whispered as he moved in and crouched beside us.

"Dallas is in trouble."

"Red Harper?" Wallis gave a low whistle and shook his head.

I nodded. Red "Tree" Harper was a big old country boy from Oregon where he'd grown up in the big timber forests, making the jungle like a second home. I could see his face; his and his One-One, Adam "Full" Nelson. The pair were inseparable.

I was about to set the team moving again when I saw the expression on Reynolds's face. "What is it?" I whispered.

"I heard Red on the radio. He was saying that he has casualties. Full Nelson is one of them."

Shit. "What did Covey say?"

"They're remaining on station."

"Roger that. Let's go."

As we started to move, Stuart asked, "What's happening?"

"Nothing. Shut up and keep walking."

He glared at me, but I ignored it. One thing I had to say for the man, he was coping reasonably well with the conditions.

We were perhaps about an hour and a half from our target when I called a halt for the night. Stuart approached me and demanded to know why we weren't keeping on. My reply was simple, "We stay here until morning." He wasn't happy about it, but I didn't care.

I waved Wallis over to me and said, "You want to do the claymores?"

He nodded but then hesitated. "What is it?" I asked.

"Just wondering why we stopped here is all."

"Dick too?" I asked.

"Uh, huh."

With a nod of understanding, I said, "The last time we came up on this village, we were on a ridge overlooking it just before dark. I then made the decision to recon it myself with my indig, Jimmy. They knew we were there. I intend on circling the village in the morning and taking up a different position."

"All right. Good idea. I'll get to those claymores."

I lay my CAR-15 beside me and waved Dick Reynolds over. Apart from myself, Reynolds, Stuart, and the two Yards were armed with the CARs. I'd insisted on an M-79 along with us, so that was Wallis.

Once the claymores were placed, we sat back and opened our MREs, filling our bodies with sustenance. Just on dark I radioed Covey to sign off. While on the air, he told me that they had eventually got ST Dallas out. Red had been wounded, his friend Full Nelson killed, along with one of their Yards. The remaining two Yards and the radio operator, Chester Lamb, had been lucky. Once I was finished, I relayed the news to Wallis and Reynolds.

Later, before we settled in, Stuart came to me. "What are you planning for tomorrow?" he asked in a whisper.

"Listen, we shouldn't be talking. Go back and take up your position."

"I want to know, Kane."

"All right. We'll move into position tomorrow and if it's all clear, Wallis and I will go down for a look. If not, we'll set up an OP and observe. Listen, on this one you're a strap. I'm in charge. If something happens to me, then either Wallis or Dick will take over. If not them, the Yards. They'll get you out alive. Alright?"

"Alright."

***

It was the silence that woke me. Of a night when the jungle is dark, it comes alive. But when something is moving around out there, things become deathly silent. I felt a hand reach out to wake me, but I grabbed it to let the owner know I was already awake. Dick Reynolds put his mouth close to my ear and whispered, "We've got movement. About fifty yards out."

I grabbed my CAR-15 and rolled slowly over. We'd all gone to sleep in our wagon wheel formation. Reynolds was on my right. At first my ears strained to hear anything, the silence being so loud, but then I heard it. Somewhere to our front, a twig snapped.

Easing my weapon further forward I slipped my finger through the trigger guard. I knew no one would fire unless I gave the order or fired first.

The silence descended again. We waited for something to happen. Then we heard the voices. Vietnamese voices. Not loud, but loud enough for any well trained SOG man to realize that they had no idea we were there.

With that knowledge I breathed a little easier, but I was still aware that they could possibly stumble upon us. And if they did, it was mission over.

The voices faded until we couldn't hear them anymore. We did, however, remain on alert for the next thirty minutes just in case. By that time the jungle had come alive once more. Some of us could sleep again.

***

We broke camp the following morning and moved towards the village. Three hours later, we achieved a suitable position after changing multiple times.

The village was occupied. As we watched it, we picked out Americans and Vietnamese. It looked as though that was where they were manufacturing the drugs and were getting ready to transport a shipment.

At one point I picked out the guy from Mama San's. However, there was no sign of General Tuan Pham until later in the day when he arrived with two trucks to transport the drugs.

It took them just over an hour to load them and then they appeared to be ready to leave. I looked at Stuart. "We need to follow them as best we can."

"How?"

"Covey."

Stuart nodded. "All right."

I slid over to Dick Reynolds and said into his ear, "Tell Covey we have a job for him."

"What's that?" he whispered back.

I told him the plan and he nodded his understanding.

"Tell Covey to standby. Once the trucks leave, radio it in and give the direction."

We waited in silence for the next hour before the trucks actually left, Pham with them. I heard Reynolds radio it in and then we waited once more.

Two hours later, Reynolds handed me the handset with a pissed expression on his face.

"Python Two this is Delta One-Zero, send."

"We lost them, Delta One-Zero."

"Say again, Python."

"We lost them in the triple canopy. There's a road down there somewhere but we can't find it."

"Roger, Python, standby."

I motioned the others over to me. "They lost the trucks," I said in a low voice.

The news was met with muttered curses from some and stony silence from others.

"The question is, what do we do now?"

Wallis gave voice to what we were thinking. "Prisoner snatch."

I nodded slowly. "That would be the next logical step. But we can't take one of the Americans. It has to be a Vietnamese soldier. Less likely to be missed and worried about."

They all agreed.

"Python Two, this is Delta One-Zero, over."

"Read you, Delta One-Zero."

"Change of plans. We're going for a prisoner snatch. We'll need air assets ready to go if we get into trouble, over."

"Will have them spun up on the launch site, Delta One-Zero. Good luck. Out."

I gave the handset back to Reynolds and said, "All right, let's do this."

***

It took two hours of silent moving to get into position to execute the prisoner snatch. Myself and Wallis were the ones who would complete it along with the Yard named Minh. We worked our way down to the edge of the village without any trouble which confirmed my suspicions that they knew we were coming on the first mission.

For thirty minutes, we hunkered down in the undergrowth and watched. Then at thirty-one minutes an opportunity presented itself.

The Vietnamese soldiers were dressed in drab green uniforms much like we were. So when a single soldier came our way, we sent Minh out to meet him.

At first the soldier was wary but after a quick succession of sentences, the soldier seemed to relax. That's when we had him.

By the time we took him back into the jungle, he was out cold.

"We need to question him," Stuart said.

I shook my head. "No, not here. We wait until we get him back."

"What if he doesn't know shit?"

I sighed and waved Trai over to me. "Ask him where the drugs are going."

Trai asked the question and right away the soldier's face changed. He knew, and he knew I knew he knew. "Ask him again?"

Trai repeated the question, only this time my knife was in my hand and pressed against our prisoner's throat. He began to blurt out an answer when I clamped a hand over his mouth. "Quietly or I'll cut your fucking throat."

I waited for Trai to translate then took my hand away slowly and I gave a slight nod. The whispers were urgent and at one point I had to put my hand back over his mouth. Once he was finished, I looked at Trai and asked, "What did he say?"

"They go to Tan Son Nhut."

"The airbase?"

The Yard nodded.

"When?"

Trai repeated my word and the soldier answered. "Two days."

I looked at Stuart. "We need to get back."

"Yes, we do."

"Dick, get covey on the horn. Tell him we need to get out of here ASAP."

"What do we do about our friend here?" Stuart asked, indicating with his hand.

"We take him with us."

We moved out and kept on until we reached an LZ just before dark. A King Bee picked us up and we flew back to our launch site.

***

There were just the three of us. Me, Stuart, and Hollister. The next step was deciding what to do. It was easy to come up with, really. We had to be in Tan Son Nhut to learn more. "I'll have a team ready to go," Hollister said firmly.

I glanced at Stuart who did the same to me. It looked as though the same thoughts were on both our minds. The general picked up on it and asked, "What is it?"

"You need to hold off on the troops," I told him.

He looked confused. I'd realized early on that Hollister was one of these go get 'em types.

Stuart said, "We need to follow this shipment all the way. If we pick it up in Tan Son Nhut then we lose that edge."

"Give it a couple of days," I said, "and have a hatchet force sent in and pick up the people at the village."

"What if you lose it?" Hollister asked.

"It's a chance we need to take," Stuart replied. "But if we can shut it down both ends, it'll be even more beneficial. Although I think the bigger fish are back home."

Hollister nodded slowly. "All right, we'll do it that way. Good luck, gentlemen. Keep me informed."

***

We arrived at Tan Son Nhut air base the next day. Stuart already had a team on site keeping an eye on things. So far, they hadn't seen anything untoward. Stuart and I replaced them and while we waited for something to happen, we tried to narrow down just how they might be getting the drugs out of the country. Afterall, Tan Son Nhut was a damn big piece of real estate.

"What would be the best way to get drugs out of a damned air base?" Stuart asked aloud.

"It would take a lot of links in the chain," I pointed out. "Everything gets checked except—"

"What?"

"I'm thinking the repatriation coffins."

"That would take some doing," Stuart said.

"They're the CIA. They have eyes and ears everywhere."

Stuart nodded. "All right, let's say they do. What then?"

"From what I've heard the remains are shipped either to Dover or Travis depending on whether they go east or west."

"That's correct."

I opened the door of the vehicle we were sitting in. "Where are you going?"

I looked at Stuart and said, "Talk to dead people."

***

"Sergeant," I said to the thin-faced man in front of me, "when is the next repatriation flight going out?"

"Sir?" The man looked at me quizzically, not understanding what I was asking.

"I'm not a sir. I rank the same as you. My friend and I would like to know when the next repatriation flight goes out."

"I just can't give out information to anyone. Sorry."

"Sergeant, my brother is on one of these flights and I want to know which one he's on."

"Brother?" he asked skeptically.

"Yes. Name of Smith. First initial R."

For a moment I thought he was just going to stonewall us again. Instead, he said, "There's two going out, sir. One this afternoon and the other one tonight. I'll have to check to nail it down for you."

"He should be flying California if that helps?"

"Both flights are headed to Travis, sir. The one to Dover doesn't go out until tomorrow night. I'll just go and look it up."

I raised my hand. "Forget it. It's fine. Thank you for your help."

We walked off and left the sergeant scratching his head. I glanced at Stuart and said in a low voice, "That was easier than expected."

"How do you figure that?"

"We come back tonight and watch. I figure they're going to do it under the cover of darkness. So if it's not tonight, then it'll be tomorrow night."

"Let's hope we can come up with something."

So we watched that night and came up empty, nothing to give us any indication of illegal practices. The next night, however, proved to be a jackpot. As the aluminum coffins were being loaded, two trucks pulled up next to the plane. Six men climbed out. All were Vietnamese. Only one was General Tuan Pham.

"Well look what we have here," I said softly as he climbed out of the truck.

"Looks like you were right," Stuart said to me.

"Educated guess."

While we watched, the two trucks were unloaded. Both had in them two aluminum coffins.

"That's where the drugs are at," I said.

Stuart nodded. "Yes. Did you see who the man in charge of the loading is?"

I stared harder and then it dawned on me. It was the sergeant from the day before. "Shit, it's our old friend."

"Yes, Sergeant Helpful," Stuart acknowledged. "You got any ideas on what we do next?"

"Yes, but you're not going to like it."

"Speak."

"We need to take that plane back to the States."

"What do you mean?"

"Hitch a ride. By the time we get back there the drugs will be long gone. It's the only way if we want to shut down the other end."

"What about Pham and his men?"

"You any good with that weapon of yours?"

"Passable."

"Come on, you'll need to be."

We came out of cover and walked towards the plane. As we approached, the sergeant I'd spoken to the day before looked in our direction. He stiffened but when he saw who we were, he relaxed. Pham on the other hand, did no such thing.

"What do you want?" he snapped.

"It's all right, General," the sergeant said. "I was talking to these men yesterday." He looked at me and said, "I couldn't find the name on the list. Maybe he hasn't been processed yet."

I nodded sadly, feigning frustration at not being able to locate my loved one. "Fine, I'll see what I can come up with."

"Go away," the general snapped.

I ignored him and walked over to one of the coffins they'd just unloaded from the closest truck. I placed my hand upon it and straight away the Vietnamese soldiers with Pham reacted, bringing up their guns to point in my direction.

"Whoa! What the fuck are you doing?"

They started shouting at me to move away from the coffin. I raised my hand and backed away. The sergeant moved in front of me and raised his hands. "Take it easy!" he shouted. "General, tell your men to stand down."

Pham stepped forward. He barked out orders in Vietnamese and his men started to lower their weapons. His savage gaze fixed on me once more before he snarled, "Go away. You are not wanted here."

My gaze hardened. "Why, General? Is there something you don't want found?"

His eyes flickered.

My hand fell to my side as I said the next words. "Like a shitload of drugs, maybe."

As his mouth opened, my hand was already moving. The M1911 handgun was in my fist and coming up in swift movement. It crashed as soon as it came level, flame spurting in the darkness. The bullet punched into the general's chest, and he fell hard.

I changed my aim as the general's soldiers started to react. The weapon I held fired twice more and a second victim tumbled to the ground.

By now Stuart was firing as well and another soldier fell.

Things really escalated from there, getting a lot worse before they got better, and before long the apron was looking like some wild west shootout – except everyone had semi-automatic weapons. By the time it was finished, all the Vietnamese soldiers were down as well as the sergeant I'd talked to the day before. Stuart was bleeding from a flesh wound to his arm and I had a couple of extra holes in my uniform.

No other American personnel were injured during the exchange, the sergeant having been shot by one of the Vietnamese soldiers.

Stuart and I had dropped our weapons and were sitting under armed guard when the base commander as well as the MPs had appeared. The officer, whose name was Derrick, took one look and exploded. "Holy motherfucking shitballs! What the fuck happened here?"

One of the men loading the plane stepped forward. "These two here, sir. They did this."

Derrick's irate gaze settled upon us, and I could feel my skin start to melt from the heat. "You two?"

Stuart said, "Might I explain?"

"Who the hell are you?"

"Smith, CIA," he lied.

"Well, start explaining, son, I'm all fucking ears."

"What I'm about to tell you sir, is highly classified

and—"

"Not what I wanted to fucking hear," the officer growled.

"Check that coffin over there, sir," I snapped.

"And you are?"

"Working for him, sir."

"Well, that's just frigging dandy."

"Look in the coffin, sir."

He glared at me before waving at an MP. "Open that son of a bitch up."

The MP stepped forward and hesitantly placed his hand on the lid, pausing.

"Just open the son of a bitch," the officer snarled.

The MP did and I've never seen a man's eyes get so wide before.

Two hours later, we were aboard that plane and headed for the States.

THE PRESENT...

"You look confused, son," Stuart said to Kane.

Kane looked across at the old man. He'd thought him to be asleep, but he obviously wasn't. Opening his mouth to speak, no words would form, and he remained silent.

"Come on, spit it out." The old man sat up and rubbed his face, focusing his attention, on Kane.

"You shot a South Vietnamese general and they let you go?"

Stuart nodded. "You're missing the point. He was a dirty son of a bitch. The base commander at Tan Son Nhut saw no issue with it after we told him they were shipping drugs in those aluminum caskets. Besides, it was your granddaddy who shot him, not me. Shit, he shot most of them bastards."

"So then he just let you fly out?" Reaper asked incredulously.

"The base commander?"

"Yes."

"Yes."

"What was the plan?" Kane asked.

"We didn't really have one."

Kane nodded.

"How well did you know him, son?" Stuart asked.

"Well enough, I guess, at least I thought I did."

"Did you know that after the war he came and worked with the CIA?"

Kane stared at Stuart. As far as he'd known, his grandfather had stayed in the military until he'd retired.

"I'll take that as a no."

More silence.

"I told you I knew him some after the war. Well, that's because we worked together. Mostly in Europe trying to stop the Russians doing what they were doing. Occasionally we'd slip across the border in Berlin and bring someone out."

"I never knew that."

"Not many people did."

Sara appeared. "Is everything all right?"

Kane nodded. "It's fine."

"You two should really get some rest, we're being flown out of here in five hours."

"Where to?" Kane asked.

"Vietnam."

Kane frowned. "What for?"

"That's where the Kowloon Triad get all of their drugs from. Cal here knows all about their operation, and we have a team on the ground ready to take them out."

Kane turned to stare at the old man. "This is all linked to the drugs which came out of Vietnam during the war?"

Stuart shrugged.

"You like playing games, old man," Kane growled.

"Adds to the excitement," Stuart replied. "This

old man ain't got much time left so I have to enjoy it while I can."

"How about you save us a lot of time, Cal, and tell us what you know," Sara said in a stern voice.

"Not until I get to Vietnam."

Kane frowned. "Wait, you've known we were going to Vietnam all this time?"

"Didn't anyone mention it to you, son?"

"Not a frigging word."

"Adds to the mystery, doesn't it?"

Kane shook his head and tossed the diary on the sofa. Stuart gave him a concerned look. "What are you doing?"

"I'm done, old man. No more reading and no more fucking games. I'm getting some sleep. If we're catching a plane in five hours, I suggest you do the same."

Stuart grunted. "Maybe I was wrong about you, son."

"Maybe you were."

***

They were up three hours later ready for the run to the airport. MI6 had organized three vehicles for the trip. Every man and woman in it would be armed and working under diplomatic status. Not that it mattered much if the Chinese wanted you bad enough.

The small convoy pulled onto the street and began moving swiftly away from the safehouse. They all fell into line and took the first corner at speed.

In the middle vehicle, Kane sat in the back with Stuart. They had taken the precaution of putting a vest on the former CIA officer just in case. Kane,

Sara, and the driver, a former special forces operator called Hansen, each wore tactical armor and carried MP5s.

For the first five kilometers everything went according to plan. Then a call came in from the third SUV. "Sara, we've got a tail."

"Copy. What are we looking at?"

"Three, possibly four vehicles."

She swore. "How the hell did they find us?"

Kane picked up his MP5 and said, "That doesn't matter. The question is what are they going to do?"

"Jerry, are you there?"

"Roger," the voice from the lead SUV came back. "We've got a tail and—"

BOOM!

Behind them the third SUV exploded, enveloped by an orange ball. Its rear end lifted into the air from the impact of a shoulder launched missile originating out the sunroof of one of the following vehicles.

"Shit," Kane growled. "Get down, old man."

"Seems I'm destined to spend my last days on the floor of a frigging SUV," Stuart snapped. "Give me a frigging gun, will you?"

"Just get down."

Suddenly the back of their vehicle was being peppered by bullets. Kane heard Sara snarl into her comms, "Turn right up here."

Both remaining vehicles took the right hard and fast. Kane felt the force of the turn and grabbed hold of the seat to keep himself stable. Through the rear window he saw the vehicles follow. Four of them. That equated to anywhere from sixteen to twenty shooters.

"Is this the triad?" Kane called out.

"Yes."

"You need to radio this shit in and get us help," Kane called to Sara.

"We are the fucking help."

"We need to get off the street," Kane said. "Make them meet us on our terms."

"Where do you propose we do that?"

Kane looked out the window to his right. He saw a sign. "There."

"The old housing district?" she queried.

"That'll do."

"It's taken over from the walled city after it was demolished. In there are criminals, drug dealers, homeless, destitute people, discards. The buildings are packed in tighter that cans on a supermarket shelf."

"Then let's use that to our advantage. It'll be like fighting in a concrete jungle."

"I hope you're right," Sara shot back at him. Then into her comms. "Jerry, turn right. We're going to make a stand."

***

The doors of the two SUVs were flung wide open as the vehicles came to a stop. Lying beside the second one was the driver who'd been cut down by a volley of fire when the Triad shooters arrived.

Around their vehicles was a different story. Four of them were down, their black suits wet with blood from the holes punched through the thin fabric. Three were dead, the other was trying to drag himself away from the firefight, leaving a red smear in his wake.

"These clowns look like they're going to a black-tie supper somewhere," Kane growled to Sara as he loaded a fresh magazine into his MP5.

They were sheltering behind a large trash bin, Stuart sitting beside them, frustrated that no one would give him a gun.

Kane came up and fired off a short burst from his weapon. A shooter who'd been sheltering behind a drum appeared, startled by the sudden pounding of the bullets into his cover. As soon as the man showed himself, Kane put one into his head.

Sara said, "They're going to try and flank us; we need to move, now."

Kane nodded. "Experience, I like it."

"Two tours in Afghan will do that to you."

Kane glanced around and saw a long, narrow, trash-strewn alleyway which led into the bowels of the Kowloon slum. It was made into a concrete canyon by the towering high-rises either side with unfenced balconies littered with rubbish and laundry.

"I guess we're going that way," he said with a resigned shrug.

"You could be right." Sara turned her head. "Jerry, on me."

The MI6 officer left his cover behind some crates and ran over to where they were sheltered.

"What's up?"

"Take the package and Pat. Head into the alleyway. We'll be right behind you."

"On it."

He helped Stuart to his feet and said, "Keep your head down, mate. Don't want a bullet parting that gray hair of yours."

"Just give me a damn weapon, son; I can help

out."

"You let us worry about that. Just concentrate on staying alive."

Letting loose with a string of muttered epithets, he allowed himself to be guided into the alley by the two MI6 men while the others lay down covering fire.

"Time to go," Sara said to Kane.

"I agree," he replied before firing another burst at a triad shooter.

They broke cover along with Colin, the last MI6 officer who'd remained with them, and as he crossed the ground between cover and the alley, a triad shooter who was already flanking them, opened fire.

Colin stiffened and fell forward. "Colin!" Sara called out and crouched to check him.

Kane turned and began laying down fire to cover her, concentrating on a shooter who was moving up on their right. He fired a burst and saw the man fall, squirming on the ground.

"We need to get out of here, Sara," he stated the obvious over the gunfire.

Sara picked up the fallen officer's weapon. "Come on, he's gone."

Sprinting towards the alley mouth, they disappeared inside, quickly catching up with the others. Jerry looked at them and asked, "Where's Colin?"

"He's dead," Kane answered for her.

"Shit," was the pissed retort.

"Keep moving," Sara told him.

Kane looked up the walls of the man-made canyon, amazed at the light that managed to get down to where they were. "Turn right here," he heard Sara order.

They turned into another, even narrower alley-way. This one was filled with all manner of detritus, including human. Kane remained at the corner, preparing to face the oncoming triad horde. Behind him he could hear the MI6 officers shouting at some civilians, urging them to get inside.

The triad killers appeared as though they were pouring through a funnel. Kane flicked the fire selector to single shot and started firing well placed rounds.

It didn't take long for them to back up hurriedly. Three more of their shooters down, two hard.

Kane whirled around to follow the others. "In here," Sara called to him.

He followed her through the door into a small foyer. There was trash scattered around the floor and the elevator was taped off. It reminded Kane of a post-apocalyptic movie complete with the graffiti on the grimy walls. It was as though the Hong Kong government had just written off this part of the city for another day.

"All this area is marked for demolition two months from now," Sara told him.

"Not too soon if you ask me."

They found the stairwell and ascended five floors, Kane covering their six as they went. It appeared to them that the triad shooters had backed off. When Kane caught up to the rest of the team he said, "Looks like we're clear for the moment."

"That's a relief," Sara replied. "But I doubt it'll hold. They've probably called for reinforcements."

"What about the Hong Kong police?" Kane asked,

perplexed at the affairs of the area.

She smiled at him, and it was the first time he'd noticed just how pretty she was, even with her dark hair pulled back in a ponytail. "Hong Kong police don't come in here. The last time they did, several of them disappeared. Word is, when they knock this place down, the PLA is coming through first to clean it out. Before that there will be a total media blackout."

Kane looked at Stuart, noting that he looked quite buoyant with the adventure. "How are you doing, old man?"

"Better than you," he shot back.

"Anytime you can come out of a gunfight still breathing is a good day."

"Yes, sir, it is."

Sara pulled Kane aside. "I'm open to ideas if you have any?"

Kane thought for a moment. "Do an ammo check and see if you can raise anyone who can help. We'll take five while you do that."

A door opened along the hallway and a longhaired, unshaven man appeared. Naked from the waist up, his bottom half was clad in baggy pants. His torso was a mess of ink, many of the tattoos graphic images of skulls and snakes, along with blocks of Chinese writing. He stared at them for several moments before retreating inside.

"That's not good," Jerry uttered to Kane.

"Why is that?"

"This area is run by two gangs, both of which are nasty. A tossup between the bad and the ugly – there's nothing good here. Another reason why the

PLA are going to have to come in. Right now, you can bet your balls he's in there calling his friends."

"Then we'd better get moving."

"I can't get a signal out of here," Sara said stuffing her cell into her pocket. "It's like we're in a dead zone."

Kane nodded. "Let's keep moving."

For the next twenty minutes, they made their way up an additional four flights which was two levels, before crossing to another stairwell. Then they went up one more story. On that floor, they found an empty apartment, tiny as it was, barely able to hold them all. At least it was somewhere for them to take shelter away from prying eyes.

"How are you doing, old man?" Kane asked Stuart.

"I'm not dead yet."

"Try to get some rest, this isn't over by a long sight."

Once more Sara issued orders to her people and then pulled Kane aside. "They can't get anyone to help us for at least another three hours."

"By then we'll have gangbangers and triad crawling all over us."

She nodded. "That's just it. They couldn't get in here anyway. We'd need to go to them."

"I have movement on the stairwell," Jerry said in a quiet voice.

Kane checked the magazine on the MP5 before peering around into the hallway. Jerry had been right. Someone – or several someones – was definitely making their way up the stairs. He slipped back out of sight, looking at Sara and said, "We can't afford to make a noise."

"What do you propose we do?" she asked, looking from Pat to Jerry and Reaper.

Kane eased his way past her to what served as the kitchen. A grimy toilet sat beside the kitchen bench, and he grimaced at the way some people were forced to live. He checked inside a half open drawer, pulling it open all the way. There in the bottom lay a kitchen knife alongside a bent spoon and some bamboo chopsticks amongst cockroach- and mouse-droppings. The blade was rusted but looked to have a reasonable edge. He picked it up. "This will do."

"What are you going to do with that?" asked Sara.

"You'll just have to wait and see."

Kane took the four steps across the room to reach the doorway. Once more, he peered around the corner. The whole way was clear. But he could still hear people making noises as they came up the stairs. He looked at Jerry. "Watch my back from the other direction."

Kane eased out the door and along the hallway. He'd made it halfway when he stopped and eased into a recessed doorway. It wasn't long before someone appeared. Obviously not a Triad shooter, this person was long haired and wore ratty jeans and no shirt, leaving exposed his heavily tattooed torso. In his hands he carried an AK47. Behind him appeared another shooter who was similarly armed.

Kane steadied his breathing, waiting for them to get that much closer. He could hear their footfalls on the stinking carpet. A few more steps and the first shooter was almost level.

With swift movements, Kane leaped out into the

hallway, the knife plunging down into the neck of the first shooter. Blood began spurting over the wall in hot and haphazard pattern, leaving a bizarre mural that would be impossible to remove.

Dropping his weapon, the gangster clutched at his throat, the pulsing blood leaking between his fingers. He slumped to his knees, the life ebbing away on a warm current. The shooter behind seemed frozen in shock, the brutal death of his companion totally unexpected, and he was painfully slow to react. He finally brought his weapon around to fire, but by then, Kane had already slashed a deep wound in his throat.

The gangster dropped beside his friend. His body spasming as he bled out into the carpet. Kane came to his feet, ready to face any unexpected threats. But the passage was clear.

He glanced back over his shoulder and saw Jerry standing in the doorway. "Give me a hand to get them inside."

Jerry emerged from the room bent down beside Kane and grabbed one of the bodies. They each dragged one into the apartment where they were holed up, taking up more of the limited space they had.

Sara gave a nod of satisfaction. "That's one way of doing it I guess."

Kane inclined his head towards the bodies. "It won't be long before they will be missed. Which means we need to get out of here now."

"Already?" Stuart growled. "I was just getting used to the décor and the open plan spaciousness."

"Get your ass up, old man," Kane said. "We've got

places to go."

The old man grumbled as he climbed to his feet and crossed the kitchen to use the bathroom facility. It wasn't long before they were all ready to move once more. The question was where would they go? Kane looked at Sara and asked, "Do you have any preferences?"

She shrugged. "How about Hyde Park?"

"Not today, signora."

Kane led them along the hallway, with Jerry bringing up the rear. Sara and Pat ushering Stuart along. They reached the stairwell and paused while Kane checked it for any more shooters. Once he was certain it was clear he moved them down the stairs instead of up.

When they reached the next floor landing, Kane checked the passage along that floor. He opened the door a crack so he could determine if the hallway was clear. On the contrary. There were two men, both armed, walking towards him.

Shutting the door, he turned to Sara and whispered, "There are two gang bangers coming this way."

"What do you want to do?"

"We have to keep going down."

Moving slowly, they took the stairwell down to the next landing. Kane tried the door. Once more he opened it carefully so he could see along the passage. This time it was clear. He passed through, the others following.

They found another empty apartment, no bigger than the last one, and went inside. There were a couple of chairs so Stuart could sit down and rest. Pat took up residence on the floor in the corner near the door so he could hear anything in the corridor, and Jerry went to watch out the window. Kane turned to Sara once more. "You need to get on that cell of yours and hurry those people along. Otherwise, we're going to wind up dead in this shit hole."

"I'll do what I can, but I can't guarantee anything."

"Just tell them to hurry the fuck up."

***

Sara came and stood beside his chair. She sighed. "We might get out of here for Christmas."

"No luck?" ask Kane looking up at her.

"They said they'd see what they could do." She raised an eyebrow in a resigned expression.

Kane nodded. "I suppose it's better than a best of luck."

"You sound like you've had a few of them before."

"On more than one occasion."

"You're not going to fucking believe this," Jerry called from where he stood beside the window. "Come and take a look."

They maneuvered through the tight space of the room to where the agent stood. Kane looked out the window, down into the darkened alleyway where men had started to gather. He said, "They're not triad. Which would make them gangsters."

"It looks like they're getting ready to search the place from top to bottom," Sara theorized.

"That would be my guess," Kane agreed.

Stuart chuckled. "What are you going to do now, son?"

Kane turned his head and stared hard at the old

man. "Going to do what my grandfather would have done."

"And what's that?" Sara asked.

"I'm going to kill all these bastards."

Stuart laughed out loud. "Yes, sir, that's exactly what he *would* have done."

"Which is a damn stupid idea," Sara said. "In case you hadn't noticed, there's lots of them and only one of you."

Kane grinned. "Makes it more fun that way. If you're worried about me, I'll take Jerry with me to hold my hand."

"Oh, that makes the world of difference. I needn't worry about you at all now," Sara said her voice dripping with sarcasm.

"While we're taking care of them, you and Pat get Stuart downstairs. Do you have enough ammunition?"

"We'll get by."

Kane nodded. "Don't wait for us, just get as far away as you can. Preferably out of this shithole. Once you hear the shooting, start moving. Understood?"

"Not wanting to burst your bubble, but you know they're going to come up the stairs, both stairwells, right?" Sara asked.

"I saw a fire escape further along the building. Once we draw them inside, you head down that."

Sara reached down and grabbed a fresh magazine. "You'll need this more than I will."

"Are you saying I shoot like shit?"

"Something like that."

Kane turned to Jerry. "Let's go have some fun."

"What you class as fun isn't necessarily the same

as what I class as fun."

Kane grinned, then reached into his shirt. He took out the diary that had been his grandfather's and looked at Stuart. "Look after this for me. I'm going to need it when I'm finished."

"You're a chip off the old block, son."

"Let's hope not."

"Why is that?" Stuart's face showed confusion.

"He's dead."

***

They met them on the stairwell, a handful of men coming up all armed with AK47s. Kane sprayed them with a hailstorm of lead. Screaming out in pain as bullets tore through soft flesh, bodies fell haphazardly to the concrete, blood spattering the wall.

The survivors were forced back under the ferocity of the assault. Seizing the advantage Kane pressed forward. After all, he held the high ground. As he'd hoped, the firing drew the others, and a bottleneck ensued in the stairwell.

The gangsters returned fire, their bullets ricocheting off the walls. Kane ducked as a round howled past his ear. Behind him, Jerry opened fire, his MP5 rattling loudly in the concrete shaft.

They reached the first of the fallen gangsters lying on the stairs. As Kane went to step over the bloody torso, a hand reached up and grabbed him by the leg. The man they call Reaper lowered his MP5 and shot the hand's owner in the head.

Two of the next three were already dead. The third was shot through the stomach but still alive. Knowing that they couldn't leave any wounded behind them, just in case, Kane dispatched him as well.

"You're a cold bastard, Reaper," Jerry said.

"Better than a bullet in the back," Kane growled. "Do you have any signal on your Comm?"

"I think so. Why?"

"See if you can raise Sara. Find out where they are."

The firing from below had ceased. Kane peered cautiously over the rail. Although he was unable to see any threats, didn't mean they weren't there. "It looks like we've won, for the moment anyway."

Behind him, Jerry tried to raise Sara. After a few minutes he gave up. "I can't get her."

"It must be the concrete walls," Kane said. "We'll keep moving down."

Kane counted seven more dead on the stairwell, stepping gingerly over broken and bloody limbs and splattered gore. Once they were clear of them, they continued pushing downwards. The other shooters disappeared. Maybe they were calling in reinforcements. Whatever the reason, Kane didn't like it.

Suddenly something bounced on the stairs. Kane looked down and saw a round object bobbling around. It only took a moment for his brain to process what it was. "Shit, grenade! Look out!"

The pair threw themselves backwards onto the hard rough surface, unable to reach any form of cover. Kane felt the wind explode from his lungs.

The grenade detonated with a deafening roar. A wave of heat and steel splinters tore upward towards them. Kane felt a piercing pain in his arm as a red-hot sliver of steel sliced the flesh open. Behind him,

Jerry cried out in agony. The MI6 man doubled over as shrapnel tore into his guts.

Kane felt as though he'd been hit by a truck. He coughed several times trying to get his breath back as he wobbled to his feet. From down below he heard shouts as the gangsters started their assault anew.

Putting his hand to his head which was ringing, he called out, "Jerry, are you OK?"

"I'm all fucked up, Reaper. That grenade tore my guts open."

Kane hesitated for a moment. They now had shooters coming up from below and he had a wounded man beside him. He cursed silently, knowing that he had to do something about the gangsters before he could tend the wounded Brit.

"Give me a minute, Jerry."

"I'm not going anywhere," he groaned.

All around him, the blast of the grenade had chipped chunks of concrete out of the walls. As Kane moved his feet, it crunched under his boots. Leaning over the rail he saw at least five shooters coming up towards him. "Don't these bastards ever give up?"

The MP5 came up to his shoulder and he stroked the trigger. Once more, the weapon came to life and rattled loudly. The first two shooters collapsed on the stairs, the other three back pedaling as fast as they could. It gave Kane the time he needed to check on Jerry.

Kneeling beside the stricken Brit, he could see immediately that it was a lost cause. He looked into the pain-filled eyes of the wounded man and shook his head.

"I told you I was fucked," Jerry grated, a trickle of

blood coming from the side of his mouth.

He said, "I'm sorry, Jerry," as he looked down at the ghastly wound that was torn into the big man's torso.

"Don't leave me alive for these bastards," Jerry begged with a shake of his head.

Kane knew what he was asking. To be left alive for the gangsters to find, his passing would be torturous. Far more painful than what he was experiencing now. The Englishman was asking to be finished humanely.

Kane opened his mouth to speak, but the Brit cut him off. "Don't tell me you can try to get me out of here because you know that's impossible. If you try, we'll both be dead."

There was no use arguing. Kane knew what he had to do. He stood up and pointed his weapon at the man. "Don't look."

"Just do—"

The MP5 spat once, and Jerry flopped backwards. Now Kane was mad. He dropped out the mostly spent magazine from the gun and replaced it with another, picked up Jerry's weapon and ammunition and slung it over his shoulder. Then as he set his jaw firm, he started back down the stairs.

By the time he hit the bottom, he wasn't sure how many he'd put down. He'd lost count but didn't care. They played the game; they lost. The only troubling part was that he was down to his last magazine for the MP5.

As Kane walked out into the alley, he glanced left to see the remaining gangsters running away. Therein lay the problem. He should have looked right first.

It wasn't until the cold muzzle of the gun was placed against his neck that he knew he'd made a mistake.

"Put the weapon down."

Kane dropped the MP5 and turned slowly. Two men dressed in suits. Triad. "You men come to take me out to dinner?"

"Where is old man?"

"What old man?"

The Asian hit him once. "Not very funny. Tell me where he is."

"Tell you where who is."

"Stop playing games."

"I don't know what you're talking about."

The Asian grew impatient. The gun pushed harder against Kane's head. "Tell us now or we will kill you."

"Tell you what."

The Asian stepped back but kept the gun pointed at Kane's head. His face was a mask of fury. "I'm going to kill you, you American dog."

The Asian's finger tightened on the trigger as he took up the slack, ready to end Kane's life there and then. The man they called Reaper braced himself.

Suddenly two shots rang out and both Asians fell to the ground beside Kane. He looked around to see Sara standing there with her weapon. "About time you showed up."

"Did you miss me?"

Kane picked up the MP5s from the ground and slung one over his shoulder. "Where are the others?"

"Not far away. Where is Jerry?"

Kane remained silent, shaking his head. "I'm sorry he didn't make it."

"Shit," Sara said, knowing she had no time to grieve the loss of her team member right now. "Follow me."

They emerged from the alley onto a sunlight-bathed street. Pat and Stuart stepped from a doorway a little further along. Sara said, "I got a call they should be here soon."

"How long is soon?" Kane asked.

The words had only just escaped his lips when two SUVs pulled up in front of them. Sara shrugged. "Will now do?"

Thirty minutes later, they were airborne in a Cessna citation heading towards Vietnam. Kane was hoping to gain some answers there.

GRAVESTONE, CALIFORNIA
1968...

The town was called Gravestone. Quite appropriate really, for a place that was almost dead. I pulled the American Motors AMX off to the side of the road. "Looks like this is it," I said to Stuart.

We'd followed the two coffins all the way from the Air Force Base. We were two days on the road. This was our third. "It sure doesn't look like much," Stuart said. "Maybe this is just a distribution center. Out of the way nice and quiet."

I nodded. "It would make sense."

"I figure we should wait until dark so we can get in and look around."

"At least that way we'll know what we're looking at."

For the next two hours we sat there and waited. Slowly, the sun sank into the western horizon. An orange color bathed the rugged landscape. After a further twenty minutes it was dark enough for us to move.

I moved to the rear of the AMX and opened the trunk. Inside was a bag with weapons in it we se-

cured from the air base before we left. Ignoring the
M16s, I chose to take the 1911 handguns. I passed
one to Stuart who checked the loads in it.

We left the car where it was and slowly crossed
the broken glass ground until we reached the edge
of town. There were no streetlamps which made me
think there was actually no power in the place. We
entered Gravestone from the south, moving slowly
through the narrow alleyways of the old wooden
homes. When we reached the center of town, we
recognized the truck where it was pulled up outside
a large building. There were two armed men standing close by.

"There's the truck," whispered Stuart.

"We need to get over there and have a look," I said
to Stuart. "Keep to the shadows, we'll move slowly."

Headlights appeared as we were about to move,
so we ducked back into the shadows behind the
building where we were hiding. Bright light bathed
the street as it drew closer to the truck. It slowed
before coming to a stop beside the larger vehicle.
The doors opened and three men climbed out. The
vehicle itself looked to be a new Plymouth.

But that wasn't the strangest thing. When the
three men approached the two guards, they both
stiffly snapped to attention and then saluted. "What
the fuck?" whispered Stuart.

"The bastards are military," I hissed.

"But they're not wearing uniforms," Stuart whispered.

"Come on, follow me. Let's get down there."

I moved silently as I did through the jungle back
in Vietnam. Behind me came the noise of a thunder-

ing elephant. I stopped. "Will you be fucking quiet?"

"I am being quiet."

"If we were back in the jungle, you'd be dead by now. Dumb son of a bitch. Fucking wait here."

I left Stuart there and moved silently on my own towards the building. Using the shadows for cover I managed to get up close. Around the back was a door so I tried the handle and it snicked open. I gave it a gentle push and waited for the screech to come from the rusted hinges. Relieved that that never happened, I managed to get the door open far enough so I could slip through it. The building had been converted into what looked like a big warehouse with crates stacked everywhere. Using them for cover I moved closer to where I'd heard voices emanating.

They were discussing getting the shipment into Los Angeles before the end of the week. I peered around the corner of the crates and saw two men talking to the other three.

"Our buyers are waiting for this shipment," said the larger of the three men. "It should have been here last week but instead we wait around just for it to get into the country."

"We'll have it ready to ship by morning," said a thin-faced man with long hair.

"Well make sure it is ready to go otherwise I'm going to have people crawling up my ass from everywhere. If they do, I'm going to be crawling up yours, and that won't be pretty."

"Alright, alright, I'll have it ready I promise."

"Make sure it fucking is. We're headed back to New York tomorrow; we have a big deal to close. I do not want to be back here."

So I had been right; it was a distribution center. They brought it here from the base and then split it up and sent it off to the buyers who would then recut it and sell it on the streets.

I left the way I came in; quietly. Finding Stuart standing where I'd left him, I said, "They're getting it ready to ship in the morning. We need to get one of these guys to answer some questions for us."

"But that will blow our cover," Stuart said.

"So what do you suggest we do?" I asked, a little irritated.

"The only thing we can do is follow them to LA and see where they go."

He was right so that's what we did. We waited until morning then followed the truck to the big city.

***

The set up was a large warehouse on the outskirts of L.A. complete with armed guards and high fences topped with razor wire. When we arrived, they were just closing the gates as a truck passed through. I pulled off the road behind a clump of bushes and then we climbed out of the AMX. We parted the branches just enough so we could see what they were up to. They backed the truck up to a loading gate and then opened the rear.

We watched them unload the product and then take it inside. Three guards walked the perimeter fence, each armed with M16s.

I said to Stuart, "Once it gets dark, I'm going to go inside and have a look around. Maybe take a prisoner and get some answers this time."

"Before we do, I have an idea."

In silence, I waited for Stuart to explain.

"I know a guy who can give us some stuff to put this place out of business for good."

I thought for a moment, then nodded. "Sounds good to me. Let's go see him."

An hour later, we parked outside what looked like your everyday run of the mill garage. It was anything but. The guy who ran the place was a former demolitions expert who'd served in Korea. Every now and then he performed jobs for the CIA. He was an older guy in his late fifties, with gray hair and a deeply lined face. He went by the name Harry but I'm guessing that was a lie.

He shook hands with Stuart and said, "Long time, no see. What can I do for you?"

"I need some stuff, Harry," Stuart replied.

The man looked at me suspiciously. "Who's your friend?"

"Just call him Mr. Brown."

I shook my head. *Fucking CIA.*

"What kind of stuff are you looking for?"

"The kind that goes bang," Stuart replied.

"I've got plenty of that shit," the old man replied. "How much do you need?"

"Enough to bring down a building."

Harry nodded. "I've got a few bricks of C4 you can have. That should be more than enough to do your job."

"I'll take it."

Harry rummaged around at the back of his garage for ten minutes before he returned. In his hands he carried three bricks of C4 plus detonators. He also carried a line of fuse. "This be enough for you?"

"You're a lifesaver, old man."

"Just don't do any fool shit like blow yourself up."

"I'll try not to."

Harry shifted his gaze and looked at me. "Can you use this stuff, son?"

I nodded. "Well enough to send you to the moon."

"Where the hell did you find this sonofabitch, Cal?"

"Vietnam."

"Looks like a tough bastard."

"Just don't get in his way."

"Are you going to tell me what you're up to?" Harry asked.

"Do you really want to know?"

"Hell, yes I want to know. I have to account for this shit. Langley will be crawling all over me wanting to know what's going on. And if I can't account for it, they'll probably send me to Alaska."

Stuart looked at me. "You want to do the honors?"

I nodded. "A rogue CIA group is smuggling drugs into the country using dead soldiers to do it."

"Did you say dead soldiers, son?"

"Their coffins anyway."

"Rogue CIA, you say?"

My voice grew hard. "That's right, the same pricks you work for."

"Don't tar us all with the same brush, son, we're not all bad."

"You'll have to forgive him, Harry," Stuart said. "They killed some friends of his."

I suddenly realized that this was the first time I'd thought about my team since we'd left Vietnam.

Harry held out his hand towards me. "Sorry to hear about your friends, son. I know what it's like. I lost men in Korea. It's not easy."

When I took his hand, his grip was firm. Calluses on his palms biting into mine. "The name's Harry Coleman. Yes, Harry is my real name."

"John Kane," I replied. "My friends call me Reaper."

"Pleased to meet you, Reaper."

"Are you two all done being friendly?" Stuart asked.

"Tell me more about your drug operation."

I said, "They're manufacturing it in Cambodia before shipping it out through Tan Son Nhut. They've got it all worked out. It comes into two different air bases in the States before distributing East or West. It's got to be worth a fortune to them."

"And the CIA is involved in this?"

"So was a South Vietnamese general until he met with a slight accident. Now we're working on shutting this end of the operation down."

"There has been an uptick in the drug trade here in LA," said Harry. "Lot of people been overdosing and dying in the street. Fucking hippies."

"While we were out in Gravestone last night, three men arrived. They looked either to be military or former military. They weren't wearing uniforms, so it could be the latter. However, they were talking about going back to New York for another big shipment. If we can roll this side up, then we can go to New York and try them."

"Gravestone? That place is a fucking ghost town."

With a nod, I said, "All the better for running an

operation out of."

"Well, I wish you both the best of luck. Yell if you need a hand with anything."

I shook his hand once more. My opinion changing about him. I guess not all CIA officers were shitbirds after all.

***

I stabbed the first guard in the chest twice and then cut his throat to make sure he wouldn't get back up. He let out a quiet gurgle before I eased him to the ground, laying him on his back. I wiped the knife on his shirt and then moved further through the shadows creeping up behind the next guard. Months of running missions in Cambodia had taught me how to use patience and stealth to my advantage. Which I did after I'd cut my way through the perimeter fence.

The second guard died pretty much the way the first had, in a spray of blood and a drowning gurgle. I dragged him into the shadows out of sight. As far as I knew, there was still another guard walking the perimeter and possibly three more men inside.

The crunch of a boot on gravel made me freeze. It was quickly followed by a raspy voice, "What the fuck do we have here?"

I remained still as a statue, holding my hands out from my side, the knife visible. The man behind me moved closer. That was his mistake to make. He got too close, and I whirled around fast, the knife coming up in a hard driving motion. It pierced the material of his shirt and drove up underneath his bottom rib. He stiffened and gasped. My left hand clamped over his mouth, so he couldn't call out in pain. I withdrew the knife and plunged it in again, this time into his chest.

Once more withdrew the knife then brought the hilt crashing down on top of his skull to knock him out, even though he was dying. That was the third and final guard done.

I put the knife away and drew my 1911 handgun. Moving silently, I approached the warehouse and eased the side door open and entered. The light inside was weak and cast long shadows across the floor.

Voices reached out to me sounding like a low monotone drone. I moved to where I could see them talking. Three men stood in a rough triangle. I watch them for a few minutes, picking the man that I would leave alive. Then, like a wraith coming out of a mist, I stepped out from behind where I was crouched. The gun bucked in my hand once and the bullet punched into the first of my three targets. His head snapped sideways, a spray of blood bursting from his skull. Taken by surprise, the two men with him started to move, reaching for weapons. I shot the second man twice in his chest. He cried out and fell to the ground. His arms splayed wide, losing the grip on his gun.

I switched my aim, the gun lowering slightly. I fired and the round hammered into his thigh, kicking it out from beneath him. He collapsed to the ground, a howl of pain escaping his lips. He tried to point his weapon at me, but I moved swiftly forward and kicked it free of his grasp. The motion elicited another gasp of pain from the downed man. I pointed my weapon at his face and said, "Try something funny and I'll blow your head off."

Already, beads of sweat were forming on his brow

as pain flowed through his body. He looked up at me with pain filled eyes and gasped, "Who are you, man?"

I gave him a wicked grin. "I'm the Reaper, asshole."

***

Stuart and I found a battered chair, dragged the wounded man off the floor and then tied him to it. By now, his pants leg was soaked in blood and there was a pool forming around his feet. I said, "If you don't want to bleed to death, you better answer my questions. If you don't, I'm just going to let you die."

"I need a doctor, man, you have to help me," he bleated.

"I don't have to do shit."

"But I'm going to die if you don't help me."

I nodded. "I guess that's up to you then, isn't it? Answer my questions and I'll get you some help."

"What do you want to know?"

Stuart stepped forward. "Start by telling us who those three guys were here earlier today."

"I don't know. He goes by the name of Mr. White."

"Do you always salute men called Mr. White?" I asked.

"Said he used to be a general or something," the man gasped. "That's all I know."

"What about the others with him?" Stuart asked.

"I don't know. Honest."

"Were they soldiers too?"

"I don't think so."

I looked at Stuart. "CIA, do you think?"

He nodded. "I'd say so."

Our prisoner looked impatiently at me. "Are you

going to help me now?"

Shaking my head, I said, "We're not done yet, sunshine."

"But what else do you want to know?" he pleaded.

"What was he going back to New York for? The general I mean."

The man gave me a confused look. "How do you—"

"Just answer the damn question," I snapped.

Our prisoner opened his mouth and closed it again. Then said, "I can't, they'll kill me."

Stuart stepped in close. His face barely inches from the man's. "In case you hadn't noticed, you are going to die if you don't help us."

"I can't. Please don't make me."

The man genuinely looked scared. I glanced at Stuart, who raised his eyebrows. So I shrugged and then shot the man in his other leg.

He howled in pain and jerked against his bonds. Veins bulged in his neck. Tears were running in great rivulets down his cheeks as pain started to overwhelm him. I grabbed him below the shirt collar and dragged him close, the chair coming with him. "Now let's try again, motherfucker, shall we? What is happening in New York?"

"What the fuck did you do that for?" he screeched.

"Answer the frigging question!" I shouted at him.

"All right. All right, I'll answer the question. There is a big deal going down in New York with a new buyer. If it goes through, they will ship in double what they are now."

"What's the buyer's name?" I demanded.

"I don't know, honest. I don't know."

Stuart stared at me. "It looks like we'll have to get our answers from New York. Let's set the charges and get the hell out of here."

Suddenly the prisoner's eyes widened in realization, the pain forgotten. "The charges, what charges?"

"The ones that are going to blow this place sky high."

"You're going to get me out of here, right?"

We turned and walked away from him. His pleas became screeches as we went about our business setting the blocks and detonators. Once we were done, we walked out of the warehouse, leaving the babbling man behind us.

Two minutes later, the warehouse exploded.

Considering that the CIA wasn't meant to operate on home soil, they were doing a top job. The office that was meant to be a laundry on Soho St was actually a safe house used for the monitoring of people thought to be communist threats to the country. The other side to it was that it always picked up little pieces of information that could be used later on. It was here that Stuart introduced me to a man named Clark.

He was in his mid-forties, and his hair was turning gray. I was impressed by what I saw; all the gadgets and gizmos that they had accumulated over the years. In one room there were monitors, as well as wiretaps which ran through the phone system they hooked into.

"What can I do for you, Calvin?" Clark asked, the lines reaching out from the corners of his brown eyes lengthening as he smiled.

"We need your help with something," Stuart informed him. "I'm tracing a rogue band of CIA operatives. They're running drugs out of South Vietnam and Cambodia. The guy in charge this end is calling himself Mr. White. I believe he's former military, but he may have some former CIA officers working with him."

"I believe there's been some talk about it. I think the man you know as Mr. White is called Rivers. General Harold Rivers. He was brought home from Vietnam two years ago, then promptly kicked out of the army."

"Do you know what it was for?" asked Stuart.

"Word is it was something to do with drugs. So, your man has form."

"Do you know anything about the other two men with him?"

Clark shrugged. "Travis and Bolton. Both are former CIA. Kicked out for drug use. One of them was so stoned that he shot a prisoner while he was interrogating him."

"Not unheard of."

"In the fucking head."

Stuart nodded. "I can see why that could be an issue."

"Yeah, a big fucking issue."

Stuart sighed. "Rivers is meant to have a meeting here with the buyer. They're talking big money. Have you heard anything?"

Clark shook his head. "No, I've heard nothing about a big buy at all. Plenty about some communist bastard trying to rally support down in Manhattan though."

"Do you know anyone who might? Know something, I mean?"

"Yeah, there's a guy in the Bronx goes by the name of Willie-Pete or something. If anyone knows he will. Look him up." Clark found a piece of paper and scribbled the address on it. He handed it to Stuart. "This is where he hangs out. Just watch your ass in there."

Stuart held out his hand. "Thanks, Clark, be seeing you around."

"Like I said, Calvin, watch your back. These guys play for keeps."

***

The address Clark gave us was a bar. It was called Manny's. It was filled with gangsters, pimps, and lowlifes. Right off the bat I knew we were going to have trouble. We walked up to the bar and ordered two beers. The barman was a small, rat-faced man with thinning hair on top. He also had a perpetual scowl on his face, which gave him a permanent look of disdain for his customers.

After he paid for the beers, Stuart said, "We're looking for a guy named Willie-Pete. Is he around?"

The bartender looked us up and down before saying, "Don't know nobody by that name."

"We were told he hangs out here," Stuart said back to him.

"Are you sure?" I asked, slipping a ten-dollar bill across the counter.

The man looked down at it for a moment before picking it up. He glanced over my shoulder towards a table near the front window. A young man sat there with two women. Both were prostitutes. "If he was sitting over there by that window, I never saw him."

Stuart and I nodded our thanks, picked up our beers and walked across to the table. I placed my 1911 on top of the table, and said, "Take a hike, ladies."

Willie-Pete looked up, taken aback by what had

just happened. "What the fuck you guys think you're doing?"

"We want a word with you, Willie," I said. "We can do this easy way or the hard way."

The women rose to their feet and beat a hasty exit. But Willie had a sneer on his face. "I don't believe you two know who the fuck you're dealing with."

"How about you tell me, Willie," I said.

"I'm Willie-Pete. I run this part of the Bronx. I could have you killed just like that." He snapped his fingers to accentuate his point.

I leaned forward and place my hand on the butt of the gun sitting on the table. I grinned wickedly. "My name is John 'Reaper' Kane and I'll kill you right now if you don't answer my questions."

Willie-Pete stared at me, unsure of what was happening. He looked around and caught the attention of someone I couldn't see. I caught movement out of the corner of my eye and lifted the gun, pointing it in that direction. "You want a part of this, keep coming, motherfucker."

The man looked as though he considered himself to be tough. I said, "And don't give me that fucking look. I've shit more assholes like you who thought they were tough. You aren't even the skid mark on old Willie's drawers. Now, sit the fuck down."

The man backpedaled and took a seat on a stool. The crowd who'd been around us moved back as well. Stuart said, "You're mean, Kane."

"I've had more top kicks scarier than he's had hot meals."

Stuart fixed his gaze on Willie-Pete. "We only

came here for a sociable chat. You want to do it here or outside?"

The man sighed. "Here will do. If I go outside with you two, I'm liable to turn up dead in the morning."

I stared into his soul. "You don't answer our questions and you will anyway."

His eyes darted to Stuart. "Hey, you want to keep a leash on the dog here?"

My hand shot out and I grabbed him by the throat. "Watch your fucking mouth, scumbag. Keep it up and I'll cut your damn tongue out."

I released him and he pressed his back further into the chair as he tried to put more distance between us.

"Is there a problem here?"

Stuart and I turned to see a large man, maybe in his early thirties, six-six, plenty of muscle to go with it. He stood as though his presence would serve the purpose of scaring us. I'd been in too many hairy situations to let a little old mountain scare the shit out of me.

"Who are you, Hightower?" I asked him.

"Rocky. I'm security here."

I nodded. "That's nice."

As I started to turn away, he said, "It's time you two left."

"Very shortly."

The man opened his coat to show me a handgun. I screwed my face up. Was this guy a fucking idiot or what? I raised mine. "Your eyes are obviously painted on."

His jaw dropped. "Whoa, man. You don't need that."

"Then fuck off."

He backed away.

Stuart walked around the table and grabbed Willie-Pete by his hair and dragged him to his feet. "Get up, asshole, you're coming with us."

"No—help! Help! They're going to kill me."

There's always one hero in every crowd. Usually, it's a country boy who actually has more balls than his sissy city cousins. However, not all the time. This time I was right. Some guy wearing a cowboy hat stepped forward just in time for me to hit him between the eyes with the butt of my 1911.

He dropped like a pole-axed steer and never moved.

"Shit, Kane," Stuart growled. "You know you're not still in Vietnam, right?"

"I know. If I was, he'd be dead by now."

We dragged Willie-Pete outside under the watchful stares of the bar crowd. Once out in the lot, Stuart slammed him down on the hood of our AMX. A clip up the back of his head from me and we had his attention again.

"Right, Willie," Stuart said, "there's an important buyer in town meeting with a seller called Mister White. What do you know about it?"

"What? I don't know anything about no drugs, man."

I got in his face. "Who said anything about drugs?"

His expression told me everything I wanted to know. "You did," he lied.

"Fuck off, Willie," Stuart growled.

"Now, Willie, we know all about there being a

big buyer in town," I said to him. "Just like you. We were told you were a man who knows things. What we want to know is who it's with and where."

"Oh, man, you know I can't tell you that," he bleated. "People find out, I'm a dead man."

"Consider yourself already dead, Willie. We're like the paramedics. The more you talk, the more we save you from dying."

"But—"

"Think before you speak, Willie," Stuart cautioned him.

The man sighed. "I might—might have heard about a new buyer coming into the city with a lot of money."

"Where from?"

"Atlanta, Georgia."

"Name?"

"Steele. Rupert Steele. Runs the drug trade in the city. It used to be just grass, but now he wants to get into the Heroin trade as well."

"Where are they meeting?"

"Mario's in the city. It's owned by Mario Rossi, the Italian mobster." Willie-Pete chuckled. "Great place to have it, right?"

"When?" I asked.

"Tomorrow night I heard."

I looked at Stuart and nodded. "I guess that's all we need."

"I guess it is," he said.

Looking at Willie-Pete, I said, "I guess we're done here. You can go now."

The man didn't need to be told twice. Within moments he was up and scurrying away from where we stood next to our car. Stuart looked at me with a thoughtful expression on his face. "I guess all we need now is a plan for tomorrow night."

"I guess it is."

***

"I don't like it," Stuart said. "I think it's a terrible idea."

I had to admit it wasn't one of my best, but it was all I could come up with at the time. I focused my eyes on the CIA man across from me as he stared back, as though it was crazy. "Can you come up with anything better?"

"You mean one that doesn't involve you shooting at me?" he asked.

Like I said, it wasn't my best idea. But it was an idea. And yes, it did involve me shooting at Stuart. But not to kill him. Instead, we would wait outside of the restaurant, wait for the people inside to emerge, and then fake an attempted hit on the one known as Mr. White. I would then appear, shoot at Stuart and then he would run off, hopefully ingratiating myself with the drug boss.

I never once said it was a good plan.

"What if something goes wrong?" replied Stuart.

"Just don't run the wrong way."

"That makes me feel a whole lot better."

"If I manage to get in, I'll reach out to you via phone, maybe through Clark."

"I really hope this works, Kane," Stuart replied.

"If it doesn't, you won't have to worry about me anymore then, will you?"

"I guess I won't."

THE PRESENT...

The plane lurched with turbulence and Kane looked up from the diary. He glanced over at the old man to see he was still dozing. He was about to go back to reading when Stuart said, "Something on your mind, son?"

"I was just reading the crazy idea that you and my grandfather had about infiltrating the drug ring."

The old man snorted. "It wasn't my idea, son, it was all him. Damn foolish idea from the start."

"I gather it didn't work then?"

"Oh, it worked alright. Have no fear about that."

Sara moved back along the plane and sat opposite Kane. "How are you gents feeling?"

Kane nodded. "Tired. I could do with some sleep, but I just can't manage it at the moment."

"What about you, Cal?" she said, asking Stuart.

"Little lady, I reckon I got more kinks in me than I had when I first started this thing. Maybe a few more gray hairs too."

Kane and Sara chuckled.

"What happens when we get on the ground in Vietnam, anyway?" Kane asked.

Sara said, "Cal here shows us on a map exactly where the factory is that the triad is using to make their drugs."

Kane was tired and his anger flared once more. "Why the hell can't you just tell us and be done with it, you silly old fool?"

"Damn it, son, are you dumb? Do you have shit between them ears? The reason why I haven't told them anything is because I wanted you here. This is about getting revenge for your grandfather. I thought I would give you that opportunity."

Kane looked at Sara. "Shit, you're MI6, don't you fucking know where it is at all?"

Sara shook her head. "We've been trying to nail these bastards for years. We know that their base is just over the border in Cambodia, we just don't know where. That jungle is pretty thick, you know."

Kane sighed and leaned back in his seat, just as the plane hit another air pocket. It lurched upwards and he felt his guts turn over. Suddenly, outside the plane there was a flash of blue light. They were flying into a storm.

Looking out the window, Kane saw another flash which illuminated the dark clouds. The plane lurched once more, dropping at first, and then lifting again with the wind updraft. "Looks like it's about to get rough for a little bit."

Sara nodded. "We will be on the ground in thirty minutes anyway. That's what I came back to tell you."

"Yeah," said Kane. "I'll be glad to get off this bloody plane."

***

It had just finished raining when they touched down at the airstrip in Vietnam. Puddles were scattered along the apron where the plane taxied to a stop. The door opened and they filed down the steps one by one to be met by a five-man SAS team dressed in plain clothes.

The team leader's name was Abbott. He was a tall redheaded man, possibly six foot five and broad across the shoulders. He introduced the rest of the team. Danny, Ken, Mucker, and Milo. To Kane, they all looked quite capable of taking care of themselves. When Sara introduced him to them, Abbott said, "I've heard of you. Heard about your team too. What they've done. Some hardcore shit."

"Don't believe everything you hear. Some of it's true, a lot of it's not."

"If Knocker Jensen is involved, I believe everything I hear. That bastard is crazy."

"I'm hearing you," Kane said with a broad grin.

"Are we ready to go?" asked Sara.

Abbott nodded. "We're set up at an old warehouse about six miles from where we are now. We've got everything we need. Weapons and ammunition, computers, you name it, we've got it."

"What about satellite link?"

"The boffins have taken care of that. Like I said, we've got everything."

"How about privacy?"

"If you're asking whether the Vietnamese know we're here or not, the answer is no," Abbott replied.

"Good. Let's—"

Kane heard the bullet before he saw it. It was like a sharp whistle followed by a dull thud as it impacted the old man's chest. Stuart grunted and started to sink to his knees, a red patch spreading instantly across his chest. Kane grabbed at him to stop him from falling hard to the ground.

As he lowered him to the damp surface, Abbott and the SAS men were already responding to the incoming fire. Their weapons came up as they formed a circle around Kane and the others.

"Did anyone see where that shot came from?" Abbott snapped.

"No idea," Ken responded.

"Well fucking find him." Abbott looked around. "Milo, get them in the vehicles now. Move, damn it."

Meanwhile, in Kane's arms Stuart was gasping for breath. The bullet had punched through his chest. His lungs were now filling with blood. He coughed, the spittle that emerged to run down his chin was red. He looked up at Kane through glazing eyes as his life started slowly ebbing away. "The diary, son. The answer...is in the diary. Finish...the diary."

"You'll be fine, old man. We'll get you out of here and get you some medical attention."

"I'm dying, son. I'm—" He coughed.

"Don't try to talk, Cal. Save your energy."

"Your grandfather would have been proud of you. You watch your back...son. They're after you too."

"What do you mean?" Kane asked.

Stuart went limp as he finally died from his wound. The old man's face looked pale, ashen, even.

"We need to get out of here," said Abbott. "Leave him, he's dead. Get up."

Kane glared at the SAS man. "I'm not leaving him here."

"Danny, Milo, get him in the back of the SUV. That fucking sniper could be out there still. Hurry it up."

Kane watched as they placed Stuart's body in the back of the second SVU. He felt a hint of sadness for the old man because he was the only link to his grandfather and he knew what had happened. Then he remembered what Cal had said about finishing the diary.

"John, we need to go," Sara urged him.

They climbed into the first SUV. Abbott followed them and got in behind the wheel. Kane felt a surge of anger flow through his veins. "How the hell did they know we were coming? Tell me that."

Abbott floored the gas pedal and the SUV lurched forward. "It wasn't from our end I'm telling you that right now."

"Well, it had to have come from somewhere. He didn't just wave a magic wand and fucking appear."

"I'm amazed the shooter didn't just keep going," Abbott replied. "We were sitting ducks out on that tarmac."

"That's because the shooter got what he wanted. We weren't the target, Stuart was. All because he knew too much."

Kane reached across and touched the diary in his pocket. At least it was still there. "How long before we get to our destination?"

"It won't be long," replied Abbott. Then Kane heard him say into his comms, "Danny, hang back a bit just in case we get tailed."

They arrived at their destination ten minutes later. The old rundown warehouse was overgrown by vines and branches from nearby trees. There were large holes in the walls, and steel girders were aged

with the rust clearly visible. The two vehicles eased
to a stop, everyone got out. Milo and Danny got Stuart out of the back of the second vehicle and carried
him towards the warehouse.

Kane looked at Abbott. "What are they going to
do with him?"

"I guess they'll bury him out the back somewhere," Abbott replied. "You have something special
in mind?"

There was sarcasm in the SAS man's voice, but
Kane ignored it. Instead, he shook his head and said,
"I guess that'll do."

"You better come inside then and meet Peters,"
said Abbott.

"Who is Peters?" this came from Sara.

"He's the head shed on this operation."

"Lead the way."

***

Craig Peters was a tall thin man with slightly reced-
ing hair. He looked to be in his 40s, but it was hard
to tell. Judging by the color of his skin he'd been in
the tropics for a while. The sun had transformed it
to a nut-brown color; gone was the pasty white one
would expect on a man from England.

"Tell me where we're at," Peters said as he stared
at Kane and Sara.

"We lost the package," Sara replied.

"I bloody well know that. What I'm asking is why
did we lose the package?" Anger showed in his eyes.

"Because they knew what we were fucking doing," Kane growled

"Why did they know what you were doing?"

"How the hell should I know? All they've been doing since I arrived in Hong Kong is trying to fucking kill us." Kane's anger was starting to get the better of him.

"Did he give you what you needed?" Peters asked.

"No," replied Sara.

"Well, what are we meant to do now?" Peters demanded.

"He told me the answer was in my grandfather's diary," Kane replied.

"Why's it so frigging hard to get an answer from an old man?" Peters thundered. "It was just a simple bloody mission."

"If it was such a simple damn mission, then why didn't you do it yourself?" Sara demanded, her anger boiling over. "In case you haven't noticed, we lost people on this thing. Or don't you care?"

Peters stared at her for a few moments. "You're right, I'm sorry. It's just so frustrating. All right, then, what do we do now?"

Kane said, "I guess I'm going to have to go back to the diary and find the answers."

Peters nodded. "I guess if that's all we have, then that's what you'll have to do."

"First, I have something to do."

Kane crossed the warehouse to where Abbott was waiting with the others. The SAS man looked up and saw him coming. "Where is he?" asked Kane.

"The chaps buried him out back. You can't miss it."

They walked out an opening at the rear of the warehouse, which led into a large green treed area. In the middle of it was a brown mound of fresh turned earth, about six foot long. Kane walked over to it and stood in silence. His head bowed. After a couple of minutes of standing there, he said in a quiet voice, "They'll pay for this, Cal. Whoever is responsible for your death and my grandfather's, they will pay. I promise."

NEW YORK, 1968…

To say Mario's had mood lighting was a misconception. It was darker than under the triple canopy in Vietnam, ultimately, I guessed, to keep out prying eyes. The meeting went down at the back of the restaurant in an even darker corner where those involved thought they were inconspicuous. But they weren't because I knew what was happening and I was able to keep an eye on them.

White was a solid man in his mid-forties. His bodyguards I guessed to be all in their thirties. The new buyer from Atlanta wasn't anything special. Average height and build, with short dark hair. The usual. However, what I couldn't work out was he was fawning over White more than necessary.

As I ate, I watched. They ate, they talked. And once their meals were finished, they got down to business. For a full hour I kept them under observation and when they were done, they shook hands and the buyer left.

Next, it was White's turn to leave. I followed him and his entourage out the door and onto the sidewalk. As he passed through the reception area, he shook hands with Mario and bid him farewell.

What happened next, happened so fast it was almost a blur. First, there were gunshots, and then I made my move. I tackled the man known as White to the ground and then lay on top of him until the gunshots ceased. Then coming to my feet, I drew my own weapon searching for Stuart. I saw him next to a sedan further along the street. He had chosen his spot well. He was under a streetlamp, not for my benefit, but for that of Mr. White.

My handgun fired three times and then I saw Stuart turn and run. I fired off two more rounds before I turned and looked down at the man on the ground. His bodyguards had weapons drawn, but they weren't pointed in the direction of where the shooting had come from. They were pointed at me.

I raise my hands in surrender. "Whoa, guys, just think about what you're doing."

"Hold your fire, you fools," White growled as he got to his feet.

The man known as White stared at me hard and long as he tried to figure out what had just happened. "Who are you?"

"No one special," I said. "Who are you?"

"I asked you first, soldier."

I stared at him for a moment trying to figure out what he was thinking. "How do you know I'm a soldier?"

"Only a soldier would react like you did under fire."

"Maybe I am."

"Thanks for what you did there."

I shrugged and said nothing. I looked at his bodyguards, who were still on edge. Something told me these guys weren't military at all. Maybe CIA.

Deciding to take a chance, I said, "If I was you, I'd get yourself some new bodyguards. These two ain't much."

"How do you know that they are my bodyguards?" White asked.

"Doesn't take much. You're wearing a suit. They are wearing suits. They are carrying guns. When that guy shot at you, they pulled them out and pointed at me. Pretty fucking stupid, actually. Maybe you should get some real ones."

I was hoping I hadn't overplayed my hand. After a few long, drawn out moments, Mr. White said, "You think you can do it?"

"Are you offering me a job?" I asked.

"You would have to be better than these dickheads," White crowed.

I turned my gaze on the two men who were staring at me. Both had expressions that said that given half the chance they would shoot me where I stood. "I'd hate to do someone out of a job."

"It's alright, they can go back to the farm where they fucking belong."

I was right, they were CIA.

"The boss told us we should stay with you, General," one of the men said. "He isn't going to like it."

"Yeah, well, you're taking your orders from me now. Alright? Thanks to you I could have got fucking killed tonight. It's a good thing that this—who are you anyway?"

"Kane."

"As I was saying, it's a good thing that Kane came along. Otherwise, I could be dead thanks to you two useless pricks. Now get out of here."

"But—"

"Fuck off."

I watched the two men saunter off along the street before turning my gaze back to White. In the distance I could hear sirens slowly growing louder as they got closer. White said, "Do you want that job or what?"

"Does it pay?"

"Of course, it pays. Are you worried about money or something?"

"I'm just a grunt, remember?"

White nodded. "I can relate to that. Are you coming or not?"

"Show me the way."

We walked on the sidewalk until we reached a red 1966 Ford Thunderbird. He tossed me the keys and said, "You drive."

"Where are we going?" I asked.

"You'll see when we get there, I'll tell you the directions."

***

When we pulled over in the parking lot of a rundown warehouse on the outer edges of the city, my first thought was that it was disused, but as we drove in through the gate, a truck pulled away from a loading dock. On its side were big red letters stating, Brown's Furniture. "What are we doing here?" I asked.

"Business," came the one-word reply.

I turned the motor off and waited for him to make the next move. "Wait here," he said as he climbed out.

"You want me to be your bodyguard, yet you don't want me around, is that it?" I asked him.

He grinned at me. "I'm as safe as a church here, son."

If only he knew how close he was to getting a bullet in his head, he might not have been so smug. "I'll wait here then, shall I?"

"You do that."

I watched him disappear and once he was out of sight, I climbed out of the car and moved cautiously towards the building. Once I reached the front wall, I edged around towards where the loading dock was and climbed up.

The large door was raised just enough for me to slide underneath it. On the other side, I found large crates full of furniture. Some others were just sitting there ready to be boxed up. Chairs, sofas, large desks. Everything a household might need.

I moved slowly through the semi-dark area until I reached the doorway, which led into a larger, more spacious storeroom. Hearing voices, I crept cautiously in that direction. It was Mr. White's voice that said, "I need the shipment ready to go in the morning. Pack it all in the furniture, make sure no one can find it until it arrives. All twenty kilos."

One of the men there with him said, "We have another shipment ready to go down to Houston."

"It hasn't been paid for yet. It goes nowhere until I get the $300,000 for it. Understood?"

"Yes, sir, General."

While I was watching I saw Mr. White pick up a plastic wrapped parcel full of heroin. He tossed it in the air as though it were a toy before catching it in a single hand. "Do we know any more about what happened down in Los Angeles?"

"We're still trying to find that one out. All I know is it was a total loss. The product is gone, and our customers are screaming about it."

White nodded. "We need to find out fast because someone did it. Someone knows something."

"Yes, sir."

Knowing that things were wrapping up I slipped back into the shadows, then out under the door. I hurried across the open area to the car where I climbed back in just as Mr. White emerged. He walked across to the vehicle, opened his door, then got in.

"Where are you staying, son?" he asked.

"Nowhere special, just a rundown motel."

"Well, if you're going to work for me, then you may as well stay close." He let out a long breath. "I'm in a hotel downtown. I'll get you a room there."

I nodded. "That all sounds real fine to me, but the thing is I got no money to pay for it."

White chuckled. "Don't worry about a thing. I've got it covered. Now start the car and let's get the hell out of here."

***

The room at the hotel was huge. I don't know how much it cost but it must have been a small fortune. It overlooked a busy street, and the horns and other vehicle noises and fumes rose to meet me as I stood on the balcony. Lights shone bright as far as the eye could see. Directly opposite were more tall buildings higher than I'd ever seen before. Lights from their windows winked at me as people opened and closed curtains.

I waited until I thought White would be in bed asleep before slipping out and down onto the street, looking for a payphone. When I found one, I called Clark.

"Stuart said you might be calling. How's it going?"

"You can tell him I'm in." I gave him the address of the warehouse where all the drugs had been stored. "Give him a message for me. There is a coffee shop on the corner of 24th St and West. I'll meet him there."

"That's fine, Kane, I'll let him know. You just watch your back. Those bastards are mean."

"I'll be fine. It's just a jungle of a different color. I'm right at home." I was about to hang up when something else popped into my mind. "Before I go, Clark, listen. White isn't the leader of this thing. Someone else is behind it all."

"How do you figure that?"

"I overheard them talking last night about the boss. The CIA is wrapped up in this somehow. I'm not sure how though. But if I had to guess, I'd say whoever's in charge is CIA. You might tell Stuart to look into it."

"I'll do that. Stay safe."

Making my way back up to the room, I wasn't expecting any trouble and I didn't meet any, so I let myself in and got a beer from the minibar. It tasted like shit, but it was cold. I sat on the bed and mulled things over in my mind. White definitely wasn't the leader of the gang. So what was he? Maybe he was the guy in charge of operations making sure things got from A to B without any troubles. With his connections he should be able to do that quite easily.

I just got out of the shower when there was a light knock on the door. I walked across to it and paused. "Who's there?"

"It's Mary from the desk, sir. I have a message for you."

I opened the door a crack to make sure she was alone. She was a short woman with long dark hair that hung loose over her shoulders. Opening the door wider, I stepped aside and said, "Please come in."

She held out her hand containing a small piece of paper and said, "I was asked to give you this personally, Mr. Kane, by the caller."

I took the paper and folded it and then ran my eyes over the tidy handwritten message. Then giving her a smile, I said, "Thank you for bringing the message up to me, Mary. I hope it was no imposition."

She gave me a seductive grin and said in a soft voice, "It was no trouble at all, sir. Is there anything else I can do for you?"

"Now that you mention it, would you like a beer?"

***

In the false light flooding through the window, I sat on the edge of the bed, reading the message that Stuart had sent me. I could hear Mary's soft exhalations. She lay facing away from me, her long dark hair spilling across the pillow.

Stuart had given me the address of a small coffee place not too far from the hotel. I was to meet him there around eight the following morning, but only if I could get away. Not knowing what Mr. White had on his books for the next day, I knew I could only try.

The operation these people had set up was massive. For such a thing to succeed, it needed people in high places. White was only the tip of the iceberg. The more I thought about it, the more I was convinced that he was the one pulling the strings. Getting the stuff into the country and across it.

But to do that he needed money. And somewhere out there was someone with a lot of it.

A soft moan was followed by, "What you doing, baby?"

I glanced over and saw Mary looking at me. I held up the piece of paper and said, "Just thinking."

"Well, seeing as we're both awake, how about we make us some entertainment?"

"I'm able if you're willing."

She gave me a mischievous grin. "I'm definitely willing."

***

"Where do you think you're going?" Mr. White asked me the following morning as he emerged from his room.

"I heard there was a good coffee shop close by and was going to get some breakfast," I replied. "You want anything?"

"Don't be too long. We've got a busy day ahead of us. Actually, get me a cup of coffee. I could do with another one. Creamer, three sugars."

I stared at him. Mr. White stared back, shrugged his shoulders, and said, "What?"

"Are you going soft?" I asked him.

He glared at me. "Say that again." His voice had taken on a hard edge.

"What happened to strong hot and black?"

He nodded, understanding what I was saying. The tension went out of the air and things calmed. He said, "You know what? Fuck it get me one of them."

He returned to his room, and I kept on walking along the hallway to the elevators. A few minutes later, I was down on the sidewalk approaching the coffee shop that Stuart said he'd meet me at. It had a red brick façade, a large window at its center with the words Cabrillo's Coffee painted across it in large yellow letters.

Inside, it was busy. I scanned the room casually and eventually saw him sitting over in a corner booth. Weaving my way through the people in the tables, I sat down opposite Stuart. He looked at me. His expression was grim. "This has certainly gone downhill really quick, Kane."

"How so?" I asked.

"Your friend, Mr. White, also known as General Harold Rivers, was linked up with a CIA Black Operations group out of South Vietnam up until he was kicked out. Said Operations Group was headed up by a CIA officer who has since been disavowed."

"What was the CIA officer's name?"

"His name is Mason Crocker."

"So, the CIA knows what they're up to?" I asked.

Stuart nodded. "They had an idea they were doing something, but Mason has a way of keeping things under the radar. He's very good at his craft. As of this moment, they have no idea where he is. Except that he's Stateside somewhere. But yes, they knew about the operation to smuggle drugs. It looks like Crocker laid the foundations for it while he was in country."

"Then why haven't they picked up Rivers? Or Mr. White as he calls himself."

"They wanted to leave him in play. They follow him and if they can, they get to Crocker."

"Then what the fuck are we doing here? They already know, why are you looking at it?"

Stuart sighed. "Because it was need to know and I didn't need to know. But now that you're inside, everything has changed, they decided to read me in and this has become my operation. And you are key to every part of it."

"Fuck me."

"This is a chance to shut down the biggest drug smuggling ring that this country has ever seen. Are you in or out?"

It was my turn to sigh. "I'm already in. But if you get me killed in all this, I'm going to be mighty pissed off."

"Right, you have to see this all the way through. Nothing happens until we get Crocker. Once we have Crocker, we shut it all down."

Something suddenly dawned on me. "If the CIA had an operation working, they know exactly what we did out in California."

Stuart nodded. "They did. And they do."

"And they let it play out."

"Yes, they did. They also saw our little show last night at the restaurant. It was them that picked me up. At first, they thought the whole thing was serious. Then I explained what it was all about."

"How come they didn't know what you were up to in Vietnam?"

"I have to assume they did to some degree. But I didn't know who I could trust over there. It was something I was working on with the MPs with General Hollister. You have to remember, Kane, over there is a whole different world. Shit, men have killed their officers with fucking hand grenades just because they didn't like them."

He was right. It wasn't unheard of. "What about the story of the rogue team that disappeared in Vietnam? The ones where my team were killed in their AO."

Stuart hesitated. "That's true. At that time, I had no idea they were part of this whole operation that the CIA was investigating. All I was doing was looking into a drug smuggling operation that I believed was being run by rogue CIA officers."

"So, no one Stateside was looking into the Vietnam side of it?"

"They were 'monitoring' things. They knew it was coming from Vietnam but out of sight, out of mind. Their main concern was shutting it down this end."

"And to do that, they needed Crocker, otherwise he would just bob up and start it somewhere else," I theorized.

"Yes."

"Now it turns to us to do it. Two men."

"I have been assured that whatever resources I might require will be at my disposal whenever the need arises."

"One more thing," I said to Stuart. "To set this operation up would have taken a lot of money, and

I mean a hell of a lot. Where has that come from?"

"If they know they're not telling me. I'll do what I can to find out, but at this time you know as much as what I do."

I got up from the table and looked over at Stuart. "If that's it, I'll get back. Take the general his morning coffee."

"Just remember, Kane, I won't be far away. I'll get messages to you when I can. I'm looking at getting a room at the hotel where you are. If I can, I will get you the number. Mary seems like she's quite capable."

"In more ways than one," I replied with a smirk. "Who would have thought hotel workers were also CIA officers?"

Stuart grinned. "See, you're already starting to fit in."

"Yeah, give me the fucking jungle any day."

***

I knocked on Mr. White's door and waited for him to answer. He opened it with a gun in his hand, then stared at me and said, "Get in here."

I walked through the door and into a large open living room. Two other men were also there, both armed; my guess they were former military or CIA. "What's going on?"

Mr. White took the coffee from my hand, heard a sip, and then put it on a small table. He nodded at one of the men who disappeared into what I assume was a bedroom. The former general stared at me and said, "We seem to have an issue, Mr. Kane. Your first day on the job and already you are causing me one headache too many."

The door to the bedroom opened once more and the man reappeared with Mary alongside him. There was fear in her eyes as he shoved her roughly onto a sofa. The former general said to me, "She was caught coming out of your room this morning."

"That's right," I replied. "A man can't be expected to do it himself all the time."

"Is that all, Mr. Kane? In my line of business. No one can be too careful."

"If you don't believe me, shoot her," I replied.

The one who'd manhandled Mary was given the nod by Mr. White and reached into his coat and pulled out a handgun, placing it snugly against Mary's head.

I saw her eyes start to fill with tears as she waited terrified for the imminent shot. My face never changed. All I could hear was Stuart's voice saying to me, we have to see this through. My jaw tightened.

The man thumbed the hammer back on the handgun and looked at his boss. While he waited for the order to be given, Mr. White glanced at me once more. "Are you sure there's nothing you want to tell me, Mr. Kane?"

"Just shoot the bitch and get over with," I hissed, playing it cool with a shrug.

"No," Mary gasped.

"Mr. Kane," the former general tried once more.

I remained silent.

"Let her go already. Maybe I'm reading too much into it. Maybe it was just a one-night stand."

I watched Mary get up from the seat and slowly

walk towards the door. I hoped she wouldn't look back. She never did.

When the door was closed, Mr. White turned to me and said, "We have business to attend to. You're driving."

"Where to?" I asked.

"Someone's trying to cut in on my business, I need to talk to them."

Somehow, I knew this wasn't going to end well.

***

I eased the Thunderbird to a slow stop outside a run-down house. On the stoop were three men dressed in dirty T-shirts, watching us closely as we got out of the vehicle. I noticed that one had a handgun tucked into the side of his pants. "Who are these guys?" I asked Mr. White.

"These, my friend, are the competition," Mr. White told me.

"Yes, but who are they?"

The former general chuckled. "They call themselves the Suburban Snakes. Can you believe that? Fucking assholes. Just a bunch of thugs who have no business sense whatsoever. So, I plan to make them a simple proposition. They either join us, or they go out of business."

"What could they possibly have to bring to the table?" I asked.

"Distribution, Mr. Kane, distribution. They have sellers right across the city. I want those sellers to be our sellers. They will be anyway, but we like to give our competition the choice."

"What if they don't come over?"

"Then they won't be a competition, will they? Follow me."

We walked up the steps towards the stoop leaving the two other guys that he had with him at the car. The young man with the gun moved to stand in front of us, smiling, exposing blacked teeth from years of neglect. "What the fuck you want? Huh."

"We came to see your boss," Mr. White answered.

"He's busy, fuck off."

My left hand shot out and hit him in the throat. His eyes bulged as he gasped for breath, his hands clutching at his neck. My right hand drew my 1911 handgun and I pressed it firmly against his forehead. "You were saying, motherfucker?"

His two friends went for their own handguns and mine shifted and pointed directly at the face of the second one. "Don't think about it. You wouldn't be the first prick I've killed."

I felt Mr. White's hand gently touch me on the left shoulder. "Take it easy, Mr. Kane. We're here on business."

We stepped around the man in front of us and went inside. The odor of the house once the door was closed was putrid. I wrinkled my nose. People say that the smell of death is bad, but that had nothing on this. We walked along the hallway, which turned left, opening out into a living room. As we approached it, we could hear the high-pitched cries of a woman.

At first, it sounded like someone in pain, but when we entered the living room we could see the source of her throaty emissions. She was totally naked, facing away from the man who she rode like a bucking bronc.

The man's eyes were closed as he sucked on a joint, enjoying their coupling, totally oblivious of the nasally tone of Gomer Pyle whining to the sarge on the television.

The woman's tits bounced up and down, her eyes also closed like the man's. Straight away Kane noticed the dark rings around her eyes and the track marks in her arms.

She must have sensed their presence because her eyes opened, seeing but not really comprehending, before closing them again.

"Fuck me, baby," she groaned in her own stoned way.

I glanced at White and saw the open look of disgust on his face. He had no problem with selling it, but no time for users.

"Hey!" I shouted.

The man's eyes shot open, and he shoved the woman off his lap exposing his erection and causing her to cry out in surprise. He tossed the joint and put his hands over his groin and blurted out, "What the hell, man? What are you doing?"

"Get rid of the girl," Mr. White said sternly.

"Who the fuck you think you're talking to?"

"Come on, Jimmy, tell her to piss off. We've got business to discuss."

Jimmy looked back at them, a surprised look on his face. "Who the fuck are you, man? Who the fuck are you? Do you know who you talking to?"

"A Goddamned suburban junky. Now get rid of the fucking broad, Jimmy!"

Jimmy looked at the woman, gave a slight nod

and said, "Get out of here, Selena."

"What about my stuff, Jimmy?" she whined.

"Just get out of here. Go."

"Damn it, Jimmy. You said if I fucked you, you'd give me it for free."

"Where is it?" I asked.

White glared at me.

"He keeps it in a hole in the wall behind the picture over there." She pointed at a landscape painting which looked more than a little out of place. I walked across and took it off the wall. Behind it was a large hole.

"Hey man, what the fuck are you doing?" Jimmy wailed.

I reached inside and found a large packet. Maybe about half a kilo. I tossed it to the naked woman and said, "There you go. Have yourself a party."

Jimmy's face grew red, his anger rising. "You take that, Selena, and I'll find you and I'll fucking cut your heart out."

"Just shut up, Jimmy," I growled at him.

He made to get up off the sofa, but I pointed my 1911 at him and said, "Don't even move a muscle, Jimmy. Just stay right there."

I could feel Mr. White staring at me. I refused to look in his direction for I knew that his anger was also escalating. After all, he was the man in charge. "Get your clothes on, Selena and piss off."

She hurriedly grabbed her things and ran out. I watched her ass wobble as she disappeared through the opening. Jimmy was still angry, and his eyes bore daggers into me as he said, "You're a dead man, and that bitch is dead too."

"Are we all done here?" Mr. White asked, his anger evident.

I shrugged. "I'm done. Are you done, Jimmy?"

"Who the fuck are you people?"

"My name is Mr. White, Jimmy. I'm here to make you a deal."

"I don't need any fucking deals. Get the hell out."

The former general smiled and said, "I think you'll like this one, Jimmy. It'll benefit you no end."

"Yeah, well I'm not listening."

"I think you'll listen, Jimmy. Because if you don't, I'm going to have my friend here kill you."

The words gave him pause for thought. His expression changed and for a moment I thought I saw fear in his eyes. Gone was the panic. "A business proposition you say? I'm listening."

"I thought you might," Mr. White said. "You see, Jimmy, you're muscling in on my business. There's only room enough for one. So, what I propose is that you just stop."

Jimmy shook his head. "I knew you were full of shit from the moment I saw you. There's nothing in this for me."

"You get to live, Jimmy. Wouldn't that be a wonderful thing? And you get to keep your distribution network."

Jimmy looked shocked. "I what? You're allowing me to keep something that is already mine. You got some big balls on you, old man."

"I'm not that old, Jimmy. The choice is yours. You either die or you keep what I allow you to keep. You've got two minutes to make the choice, Jimmy. Don't waste it. Could be your last two minutes on

Earth."

Uncertainty flashed in his eyes as he mulled over the impossible position the proposition put him in. He rubbed at his unshaven jaws, as though deep in thought, but we already knew what the answer was going to be. Under that tough exterior was a chickenshit coward who would do anything to save his life. "All right, I'll do it. But what assurances do I have?"

"Why, Jimmy, you don't have any, none at all. You work for me now. Your life is in my hands. Just remember this if you cross me; I will kill you. I will not hesitate, and I won't send someone to do it for me. Do you understand me?"

Jimmy mumbled something incoherent. I waited for what was to follow. "I can't hear you, Jimmy," Mr. White said.

"I said all right." His voice was louder than it need be, but Mr. White let it go.

Instead, he looked at me and said, "Time to go, Mr. Kane."

We all climbed back into the Thunderbird and as I pulled away from the curb Mr. White said, "Take the rest of the day off, Mr. Kane. I'll need you tonight though."

I looked at my watch, it wasn't even past 11 a.m. "Really? It's not even noon and already you're giving me the rest of the day off."

"I have a meeting. I won't need you."

"I thought you hired me to take care of your interest? Keep an eye out for you?"

He nodded. "That's correct, I did."

"Then how am I meant to do that if you're giving

me days off?"

"Because I don't want you, Mr. Kane. Can't you understand that? You do as I say."

I realized I was starting to push him too far, so I backed off. "All right, Mr. White. Just trying to do my job. The one that you hired me for, that's all."

"Remember this, Mr. Kane, your job is to do whatever I tell you to do. No questions, just do."

"Yes, sir."

"Now take us back to the hotel."

***

I watched them drive away before turning and walking inside the hotel. The foyer wasn't as busy as the previous evening but there was still a good amount of people in there. I walked up to the counter and asked if there were any messages.

"What name please, sir?" the young lady behind the desk, asked me.

"Kane, John."

"Just one moment, sir. I'll have a look for you."

When she turned back, she held an envelope for me. I took it and looked at the writing on the front of the crisp white paper. I looked up at her and she smiled at me. "Thank you very much."

I waited until I got into the elevator before I opened it. All that was written on the paper inside was room 364. Hurriedly, I hit the button for floor three before the elevator whizzed past it. It stopped, the door dinged and then slid open.

I stepped out into the hallway onto a checker pattern lush carpet. Staring at my face was a painting of a half-naked woman in a state of repose on a chaise lounge. I looked left and right deciding which way I should go. I guessed left but should have gone right, but that didn't matter. I found the room eventually.

Knocking on the door, I waited a few heartbeats before it opened. Stuart stared at me before looking left and right. He said, "Get in here."

Mary was sitting on the sofa. Gone was the uniform. Now she was dressed in a pair of jeans and a white T-shirt. Her long hair was left loose hanging down at the back. She glared at me and growled, "You're a fucking asshole, Kane."

"And you are still alive," I shot back at her.

"He could have killed me, and you stood by and did nothing." Her anger was very real.

I nodded. "I was banking that he wouldn't."

"And what if he had?"

"I wouldn't have let it get that far."

"Says you. I'm not that damn confident."

I shrugged. "What's your real name?"

She was taken by surprise. "What do you mean?"

"Your real name. It's not Mary."

"Can we get on with the thing at hand?" Stuart interjected.

I looked at him. "Sure."

"And just so you know, Mary will be working with us from now on."

"That's all right with me."

"What are you doing back at the hotel so early, anyway?" Stuart asked.

"The general had a meeting," I replied.

"With whom?"

"I don't know. I pushed him as far as I could to let me go along but he still doesn't trust me enough."

"You figure it was to meet with Crocker?"

"Could be."

"So, what else have you got?" the CIA man asked.

"We went and saw a guy named Jimmy this morning. He's the man in charge of some crowd called the Suburban Snakes. White made him an offer."

"What kind of offer?" Mary asked.

"The kind that is you do as I say, or you'll be dead in the gutter before the day is over."

"Which was?" Stuart asked.

"Jimmy and his people work for him and distribute across the city."

"Sounds like they're expanding," Mary said.

My head bobbed. "If you hurry, you'll be able to get the police to wrap them up at their shit house. They keep their drugs in the wall behind a picture."

"Why would we do that?" Stuart asked.

"Shake a tree and see what falls out. Maybe if we make White look incompetent, then Crocker might surface to straighten things out. Nothing big, just little things that irritate. He comes out, we can take him down."

Stuart said, "It might work."

"We can only try."

"I have news from Vietnam."

"What?" I asked.

"A B-52 strike was ordered on the village where they were operating out of. Smashed the shit out of it. Also, Hollister started cleaning up those left over. Some slipped through his net though and they could be on their way back here. If they show, you could be compromised."

"I'll deal with it when and if it happens."

"OK then."

I said, "The standout question though is what will it do to their operation? Shutting down the pipeline will force them to find another. But where?"

"I guess time will tell."

"I have to be getting back just in case White appears." I looked at Mary. "Well?"

She frowned at me. "Well, what?"

"What's your name?"

"Alice Morgan."

THE PRESENT...

Kane looked up from the diary. "Son of a bitch."

Sara looked across at him, a questioning expression on her face. "What's up?"

"My grandmother worked for the fucking CIA." There was surprise in his voice.

"You didn't know this?"

He swatted at a mosquito as it buzzed past his eyes, his hand waving furiously. "I had no idea. I don't even know my family anymore. I can't even ask my parents if they knew because they're both dead."

"I'm sorry, I didn't know," Sara replied. "What about your grandmother?"

"She died five years before he did."

"Do you have any other family?"

Kane said, "A sister." He left it at that.

Peters entered the room with an unhappy expression on his face. "Do you have anything yet?"

His words were abrupt. Kane ignored them, and said, "Nothing yet."

"Well hurry the hell up, I'm starting to think that this place doesn't exist. A bloody fantasy of an old man's mind."

"Cal said it's in there somewhere. I've started

taking notes, so hopefully we can put something together. Maybe it's a code, who knows?"

"Maybe it's a fantasy," Peters said. "I'll give you three more hours, and if it's not done by then, I'm shutting it down."

He stormed off and Kane looked across at Sara. She gave him a sorrowful look and asked, "Don't you have anything?"

Kane opened his mouth to speak and then shut it again like a steel trap. Stared at her for a moment, his silence was deafening.

"What is it?" she asked.

"Just before he died, Cal said something to me."

"What was it?"

"He said, they're after me too."

Sara frowned. "Who?"

"I don't know. Maybe the triad?"

"None of this makes sense," Sara said to him. "We have no idea what we're looking for; where we're meant to be going. This big thing that's in this diary, that's hidden, or is it in plain sight? We don't know."

She was right. They were as oblivious to whatever they were looking for, now, as they were at the start. It felt as though Stuart had been taking them on a wild goose chase with no end in sight.

"What do you plan on doing?" Sara asked.

"What I have been doing. Reading."

***

Sara walked out the back of the building and lit up a cigarette. It was the first one she'd had in days, and the nicotine rushed straight to her brain. She blew out a cloud of smoke and heard soft footfalls stop beside her. "Did he say anything?" Peters asked. Gone was the English accent, replaced by an American one.

Sara sucked deeply once more before exhaling and then turning to face the man beside her. "Nothing helpful. Although he did just find out that his grandmother used to work for the CIA."

"I don't know why we just can't kill him before the triads find us."

"Because we follow orders. Don't you understand that?" Sara's voice was impatient enough to let her own fake accent slip.

"What does it matter?" Peters asked.

"The orders are to see it through to the end."

"I think the boss is making a mistake. He's letting it get too personal."

"He will be here later today. Then it'll be over. Until then, we follow his plan."

"What if he reads something in the diary and puts it all together?"

"That can't happen. It's been taken care of. You were careful about that, weren't you?"

There was no reply.

"Well?" Sara asked impatiently.

"Why me? I thought you were going to go through it."

"Oh for fuck's sake. Don't tell me the diary wasn't fucking checked."

"Obviously not," Peters shot back at her.

"Did the old man read it?"

"Maybe. I don't know." Peters shrugged his shoulders.

"Christ. You'd better hope there's nothing in

there that can come back on us or it's all screwed. Just like we will be."

"What was the point of killing the old man, anyway?" Peters asked.

"He was becoming a liability. I checked with the boss, and he ticked it off. It was going to happen anyway. We have Kane. He's the last piece. The part I can't believe is, how well the plan has fallen into place."

"Apart from the triad," Peters pointed out.

"And the diary," Sara replied.

"Something isn't right," Peters said. "The triad has been onto us right from the start."

"Don't worry about it," she replied.

"But they knew where we were. It's like they have ears on the inside."

"Not our problem," Sara said. "All we have to do is keep Kane with us until the boss arrives."

***

The more Kane thought about it, the more he was convinced that something wasn't right. Like Peters, he was trying to work out how the triad was tracking their every move. The answer was simple, they had someone on the inside. But who? The only ones left were Sara and Pat. It could be Peters, but he didn't think they were in contact at all.

He touched the butt of the P226 reassuringly. The other thing that bothered him was what Stuart was trying to warn him about.

However, the more he thought about it, the more questions remained unanswered. He needed to finish the diary.

NEW YORK, 1968...

I sat in my room and waited for White to come to me. It was just after dark when he did. The door opened and he walked in, no knock or anything. I stared at him, and he held up a key. "Don't look so surprised."

I'd have to remember that going forward. He was lucky I didn't shoot him.

"Come on, we're going," he said to me. "And before you ask, I'll tell you when we get there. Bring your sidearm."

I followed him out the door and down through the lobby onto the street where the same two men who were with him earlier waited beside the Thunderbird. "Get in the back, Kane. You ride with me."

"Demoted already."

"If you don't like it, I can leave you behind."

"Then who's going to save your ass when the shit goes down?"

He glared at me and for a moment I thought I'd overplayed my hand. "Let's get one thing straight, Kane. You are expendable just like everyone else."

"Understood."

"Good, now get in."

We spent the next few hours driving to Binghamton in Broome County. It seemed a long trip, made even more so by the heavy silence which accompanied us all the way there.

When we stopped, it was at a construction site where a once ornate building had stood only to be torn down and replaced by a steel monster in the process of being built.

"Get out of the car and have a look around," White ordered. "Make sure we don't have any uninvited guests."

I started to get out and he put a hand on my arm. "Not you. You stay with me."

The two others swept the area looking to see if there was anyone hiding in the shadows. The one thing I had figured out along the way was their names. Both were CIA. had to be, or former CIA. Keeping with our color scheme, one was called Mr. Black and the other was called Mr. Gray.

Five minutes later, they returned, giving White the all-clear. Then he said to me, "You can get out now."

The air had a chill to it. My eyes started left and right trying to make sure that nothing had been missed. It was a habit I'd picked up in the jungle. My head was on a swivel. If you missed one little detail out there, it could be the difference between life or death.

"What is this place?" I asked Mr. White.

"Something to do with the new initiative the city is going through," he replied. "They're ripping down the old and building up all this new monstrosity shit. It is all to do with money."

"So what is it we're doing here?" I asked him.

"We have a business deal to conduct, Mr. Kane," White replied.

After that we waited in silence for a further 20 minutes. Mr. White kept checking his watch impatiently. For a moment I thought he was about to give up and go home, but soon a set of headlights began bouncing along the street adjacent to where we were. It reached the driveway and then pulled in.

Mr. White said to me, "Keep an eye out. If anything happens, you start shooting and don't stop 'til everyone is down."

I looked at him through the darkness for a moment before saying, "Sounds like these are nice people."

"One thing you learn in our business, Mr. Kane, is that you do not trust anyone."

The black Town Car came to a stop. The lights went out and then the doors opened. Four men emerged, three of which looked to be bodyguards. They moved away from the man in the center like they were standing a perimeter. I could only assume that they were armed, but it would have been a good guess.

The man they surrounded took three steps forward before stopping. He said to the former general, "You are Mr. White, I presume."

"And you would be my buyer."

"Shall we get down to business?"

Mr. White signaled to Mr. Gray who turned away and went back to the Thunderbird. He opened the trunk and retrieved a case before walking back to where we all stood. "Now show me yours," Mr.

White said.

Another hand signal from one of the buyers and men repeated the movements that Mr. Gray just had. When their case was sitting in the right position, the buyer said, "Would you like to check the money?"

Mr. White snorted derisively. "Well, I'm not about to let you fucking drive off with it without checking it, am I?"

Mr. Gray and his opposite number strode forward, exchanged cases and then returned to place them on the hood of their vehicle. They were opened and the lids folded back. The case on the Thunderbird was full of cash, the one on the town car was full of bricks of heroin.

A lot of money and a lot of drugs. Equals a lot of temptation.

The movement was an insubstantial flicker at first. But still, an eye like mine trained to detect certain dangers in the jungle, picked it up straight away. The buyer's Number 3 man decided he would slip his hand under his coat and let it rest there.

Without taking my eyes off him, I moved, crossing behind Mr. Black. As I did, my hand slipped closer to my 1911.

I paused about a foot to Mr. Black's right. The buyer's Number 3 man was still acting a little nervously. Then I caught sight of his Number 2. A step forward and I said out loud, "Mister, I would put that gun away or I'm going to put a hole right through you."

The Number 2 man stared at me. "What did you say?"

"I said if you keep acting like that, I'm going to fucking shoot you. Understand me now?"

The buyer froze, then from beside me I heard Mr. White whisper, "What the hell are you doing, son?"

"It would seem that the buyer has other ideas for his purchase here this evening, sir," I said loud enough for everybody to hear. "I do believe he plans on taking both the drugs and the money."

The buyer looked surprised. "Are you for real? Maybe you've just had a little bit too much of this white powder go into your veins." He looked at Mr. White. "Are you buying this fucking shit?"

"I don't know. Are you trying to rip me off? Because if you are, you just made a very bad mistake."

"Now hang on a minute," he protested. "I don't know what you think this is, but I know what it isn't."

"And what exactly is it?" Mr. White asked.

"It's a business deal just like we agreed."

While they discussed the deal, I kept my eyes on nervous Number 3. His body language had changed. He was stiffer, more on edge. Maybe ready to unload like a coiled spring. He caught me staring at him and my eyes narrowed. He gave me a 'what the fuck are you looking at' stare.

I gently shook my head from side to side in warning. After all, if he was going to kick something off, people could get hurt. But alas, my warning went unheeded, and he started to bring his handgun up.

He never even got it halfway because I was ready. My 1911 roared kicking back hard in the palm of my hand. The bullet punched into Number 3's chest and he cried out in pain. His arms flailed like a windmill before he sat down hard on the gravel and dirt of the building site.

Startled, Mr. White's head spun around to look directly at me. But I ignored him because Number 2 was making his move. This time I fired twice, both rounds punching into Number 2's chest.

He was dead before he hit the ground beside his friend.

But there were still two men I had to watch. The buyer, and his main bodyguard, the one who had delivered the case.

A shot crashed out and I felt the warm burn of a bullet as it passed close to my face. I dropped to a knee and swung the 1911 to the right, its foresight centering on the main bodyguard's torso. Twice I squeezed the trigger and twice the man jerked under each impact. He staggered backward before dropping to his knees, clutching at his chest, trying to stem the blood which was leaking from the two holes I'd just put there.

The man's handgun had fallen to the ground close by, but he left it where it had landed. Moments later, he looked up at me. He's eyes still trying to comprehend that his life was slowly ebbing away. Then, like a giant tree in the forest, he slowly lay to one side before falling over onto the ground.

Turning to my right, I brought the handgun into line with the buyer. Striding purposefully forward I raised the weapon and placed it against the petrified man's forehead.

"Kane!" White snapped.

My finger relaxed only an ounce or so away from killing the man. However, I left the gun in place, pressed firmly against his head.

"Don't kill him yet," the former general said.

"Why not?"

"Because I said so."

So I waited.

"What was all this?" White asked him.

"It wasn't nothing."

White sighed and then shot the man himself. The buyer dropped like a stone to the ground and never moved.

I looked at the former general and said, "I guess our business here is concluded."

***

I was tired but Stuart needed to be debriefed so I went to his room. He sat and listened to everything I had to say and then said, "I know."

I stared at him. "What the hell?"

"There were a couple of men following you. They saw everything."

"You might have informed me about the tail," I snapped.

"It's all right, I borrowed them from Clark. He said they're his best men."

"Did they know who the buyer was?" I asked.

"John Lang, local real estate man. A lot of the work there he's tied up in."

"Then why does he need to deal in heroin?"

"You know the type, the more money they have, the more they want."

"Yeah, well he isn't going to make any more." I sighed and got up. "I'm tired."

Stuart saw me out but when I reached the elevator, I pressed the button to the lobby instead of my own floor. Once I reached it, I headed for the dining room. Just in time for breakfast.

I ordered bacon and eggs and toast. It sure beat a piss and frig all else in the jungle. It came with something called a bottomless cup of coffee. I'd never heard of one before, but it turned out that you were able to drink as much of it as you could, and they'd just keep topping you up.

"Mind if I join you?"

I looked up and saw the woman I knew as Mary standing there. Pointing to the chair I said, "Sure."

She sat down and ordered a coffee before saying, "Eventful night?"

"You heard?" Of course she had.

"Maybe," she replied sipping her coffee. "Apparently you can take care of yourself outside of the bedroom too, soldier boy."

"I've had some practice at that."

She grinned at me, showing her even white teeth. Her face was pretty, and I figured her to be around the same age as I was. It was actually the first time I got to really look at her. The other night we'd been a little bit too busy to take in each other's features.

"What are you looking at?" she asked.

"You."

"Did you learn anything?"

"Do you mean last night?"

"Something like that."

"Yes, I think I did."

"What was that?" she asked.

"I learned I'd rather be back in the jungle."

Mr. Black appeared and stood beside the table. I looked up at him and wished he would just disappear. He cleared his throat, and said, "The boss wants to see you."

"I'm still eating breakfast."

"Now means now."

I looked across at Mary and said, "I guess now means now."

She smiled innocently and said, "I guess it does."

Grabbing a piece of toast I climbed to my feet, took a bite and said, "Lead on."

***

Mr. White was sitting at a small table in his room waiting patiently for me to appear. In front of him was a cup of coffee. A second one off to the side. He pointed at it and said, "Take a seat. I got some coffee for you."

"What seems to be the problem? I was just about to head upstairs and go to sleep. I've had my breakfast. Most of it anyway."

"He was with that woman again, boss," Black said.

I waited for White to say something, but he remained silent. Instead, he sipped his coffee and placed the cup back onto the table. "We're leaving on a plane tomorrow."

Frowning, I asked, "Where are we off to?"

Mr. White contemplated his answer for a moment and then said, "We're going to Hong Kong for a couple of days. I have some business there to take care of."

"You want me to come to Hong Kong with you? Just like that."

"Do you have anything else to do?" the former general asked.

I shook my head. "When are we leaving?"

"Tonight. Pack whatever you need. And be back here. Around seventeen hundred. Have a problem with that?"

"As long as I can get some sleep, I'll be back here," I replied.

"Good, now get out of here."

"What exactly are we going to Hong Kong for?" I asked Mr. White.

Again, there was that pause before he answered, "It's a business trip. We had some problems with our Vietnam end. We need to open a new pipeline and I know some people in Hong Kong, who will—should help out."

"All right, then, I'll see you when I get back here later."

"Don't be late, Kane, or the plane will leave without you."

KOWLOON, 1968...

The streets were narrow and busy. Both with automobiles and foot traffic. The vehicle we were in crawled along, the driver beeping the horn in frustration as he tried to weave his way through the roadblock of metal obstacles.

He turned and looked into the rear seat, where both I and Mr. White was sitting. He gave the former general a toothy grin and said, "Sorry, Mr. White, fucking traffic. I will explain to Mr. Ling when we get there."

I could see why he was getting frustrated, but I think most of that was the jet lag because hardly any of us had slept on the flight. He nodded and remained silent, and it seemed to satisfy the driver. Following us in another car was the rest of our entourage. Three men, all armed with concealed weapons.

Curiously, I asked, "Where is it we're going anyway?"

The Hong Kong local, whose name was Jing, looked at the rear-view mirror and said, "To the Golden Dragon. It big hotel, many rooms, really good. Plenty girls if you want."

I nodded and he went back to concentrating on his driving.

For the next hour, we crept along like a tortoise on wheels. By the time we reached the Golden Dragon, I swear I was partially deaf from all the blasting of the horn. He pulled up outside the hotel, hurriedly jumped out, then opened the door for Mr. White.

We followed him into the lobby where we were met by a bellboy dressed in a black and white suit. "Welcome to Golden Dragon. Hope your stay is good."

Mr. White said, "Our bags are in the car, boy."

To which his response was, "Welcome to Golden Dragon. Hope your stay is good."

Jing snapped some words at him, and the bellboy smiled before scampering outside to get the luggage from the car.

We were escorted to the desk where our group was checked in under the name of Merriweather. With keys issued, we were shown to our rooms, all on the 10th floor. I walked out onto the balcony and looked down. It was like looking into a concrete crevasse below where people wandered aimlessly. Nearly every building that I saw had signs hanging out over the narrow street.

I went back inside and sat on the edge of the bed, then laid back with my feet still touching the floor and closed my eyes. I was almost asleep when a knock sounded at the door. *Fuck*.

"Who is it?" I called out not being bothered to move.

"Room service." It was a woman's voice.

I frowned and climbed off the bed, slowly walking

towards the door. I turned the handle and swung the door open. Standing before me was a slim woman with black hair which flowed down over her shoulders. She was attired in a red dress that ended mid-thigh, revealing long tanned legs. The V shaped neckline went down past small round breasts. I sighed. "I'm not in the mood, just go away."

"But I here for you."

"I don't want you."

Not taking no for an answer, she pushed past me and entered my room. "Just come on in," I said helplessly.

Her handbag was the same shade of red as her dress, and she dropped it onto a chair before turning to face me. "My name is Mae."

"Why are you here Mae?"

"I was told to show you a good time."

She started removing her dress, revealing that she wore only a pair of silky panties beneath it. I held up my hand knowing I'd regret it and then said, "Put the dress back on."

She looked shocked. "But I have to do."

For a moment I thought and then I came up with an idea. "Mae, can you do massage?"

"I very good."

I took off my shirt and lay face down on the bed. "Good. Start with that."

Exactly two minutes after she started, I was sound asleep.

***

I don't know how long I'd lain there. But I was sure it was a while. However, I was awakened rather rudely by three Asian men who looked none too happy to see me. "Get up," said the one in the middle who was obviously the leader of the trio.

"Who the fuck are you?" I growled as I started to sit up.

"I her husband." He stabbed a finger at Mae who lay beside me on the bed. She was wide awake and had a hint of a smile on her lips.

It was a setup, I'd been had. Obviously, they hung around hotels looking for patsies. I just happened to be their next victim. "Son of a bitch."

There was no way to talk myself out of it. They weren't going to let it go. It was going to end either one of two ways. Or maybe three. "I don't think you've really thought this through."

"You give us money, maybe we go away," the boss said.

From on the bed, Mae smiled. She said, "Maybe him like men, not like girls."

"Is that right?" the man sneered. "Do you like boys?"

"Maybe it's just best if you all leave." My voice was tired.

"Maybe you shut fuck up. Give us money."

"I don't have any money."

He stabbed a finger at me, his sleeve slipping up to reveal a tattoo. A scorpion. "You lie."

One of the others stepped forward and reached out to search me for what he thought would be money. Instead, as soon as his hand touched me, I moved. Sudden, swift.

My left hand grabbed his arm just above the wrist. My right elbow came down hard and fast. It hit him just below the elbow and I heard the sickening crack as bones gave way underneath the brutal force.

The man screeched in pain and buckled at the knees; my elbow shot up and back, this time hitting him flush in the face. His cries of pain stopped as he slumped to the floor out cold. From the bed I heard Mae screaming her alarm.

Without waiting for the others to respond, I moved forward swiftly. I was fully aware that these guys would be experts in martial arts, so my plan was to take them hard and fast, not allowing any time to gather themselves.

I hit the leader in the face with a clenched fist. His head snapped back, and he staggered but didn't go down. I moved in close and hit him again. This time his knees buckled, and he went down onto one of them.

His friend hit me from the side, a powerful blow that connected just above my ear. Stars flashed before my eyes as I lurched to the right. He came in closer and was about to hit me with a roundhouse kick to the side of the head to follow up the punch. I dropped to my knees and then drove a right fist into his groin as his leg swept over top of me.

He let out a sickening groan as he doubled over and fell into a fetal position. I didn't give him any chance to recover. The weapon I carried came out and I slammed it down onto the back of his head.

The interruption gave his boss time to recuperate. He came back to his feet and started to run at me while I was off balance. I brought the handgun around and pointed it at him, but it was too slow. He slapped it aside and cannoned into me. We both sprawled onto the floor.

Snarling, he tried to drive his thumbs into my eyes, but I managed to grasp his wrists before he could do any damage. My head came up off the floor and my forehead slammed into his nose. He cried out in pain as blood spurted from the sickening blow. I rolled him off me to the side and he lay there stunned.

I staggered to my feet. Somehow, he caught a glimpse of my handgun which had ended up on the floor. He rolled to the side and made a last-ditch effort to grab it so he could bring it back and shoot me. My foot lashed out and caught him in the side of the head with a sickening crunch. I'm pretty sure I broke his jaw right then.

Still on the bed, Mae was screeching like a mad parrot. I turned and stared at her, shaking my head. "Will you shut the hell up?"

Still, the screeches came, and fed up, I stepped across to the bed and slapped her hard across the face. They stopped abruptly and she stared at me in fear.

"Who are they?" I demanded.

"Xiē zi," she replied.

"Who?"

"The Scorpions. They are crime family."

Great, I'd been in Hong Kong a few hours and I'd already drawn the attention and made enemies of the toughest guys in town. I bent down and picked up the handgun, stuffing it into my waistband. I walked over to the door and opened it, sticking my head out into the hallway. "Mr. Gray, are you there?" I called out.

After a few moments, the door opened three along from my room. He stuck his head out into the hallway, glared at me and said, "What do you want?"

"I have a problem. You might want to come down here." He gave a sigh of frustration, then walked towards me along the hall.

I stepped aside and allowed him to pass, and he pulled up short as he saw the three men laying on the floor. "What the hell is this?"

"They figured they could make some easy money. They were wrong, but I don't know what to do with them now."

"I'd better get the boss," Gray muttered.

"Why bother him?"

"Because these are the pricks we're coming here to do business with."

***

Jing looked at the three men who were now sitting up. The one with the broken jaw looked to be in the poorest shape. Not that anyone cared. He walked up and down, berating them before he turned away and looked at Mr. White. "I am sorry, Mr. White, so sorry. Mr. Ling will hear of this, and he would punish them accordingly."

White looked at me and then back to Jing. "I'm sure they've seen the error of their ways. What I need is answers about what's going on with my meeting with Mr. Ling."

"Yes, Mr. Ling sends apologies he has been held up with another matter. But he assures me that he will get to see you tomorrow."

White wasn't happy. "So, what am I meant to do

in the meantime?"

Jing smiled. "You are in Hong Kong. Enjoy the city. Become tourist."

After Jing and the others had left the room, Mr. White swore out loud. "I'm a businessman, not a fucking tourist."

No one said anything, but then he turned his gaze upon me. "I'm beginning to think that having you around is not such a smart idea. Do you always get into this much trouble?"

I straightened and stuck out my chin. "I don't go looking for it if that's what you mean."

The former general let out a sigh and then gave a slight nod. "Fine, fine. I have to reach out to the boss and let him know what's going on."

For a moment, I thought I'd chance my hand. "Who is the boss?"

"Someone you don't need to know anything about."

I left it at that.

***

I had a feeling it was bound to be one of those days. It might actually have had something to do with the five guys standing before me. But wait, let me go back.

After my indiscretion earlier that day, I decided to go out and have a look around. After all, nothing was going to be happening before the next day. So I wandered the narrow streets of downtown Kowloon. Which in fact was quite an eye-opening experience. Found a place to have coffee. I even found an American bar. Crazy. Sitting there I had a couple of beers before deciding to return to the hotel.

But somewhere along the way, I got lost. I was about the only one that was. The guys with the scorpion tattoos certainly weren't, especially the one with the broken jaw. Obviously, he was that hopped up on drugs, his eyes glazed over. However, he wasn't the one that did the talking. This was left up to a much taller guy, much broader across the shoulders.

I had my handgun but didn't really want to use it, but if I was going to save my life then I might just have to do that. I held up a hand and said, "I don't want any trouble."

"It's a bit late for that, don't you think?" the tall man said in almost perfect English. I think I even detected a hint of an American accent.

"Listen, I'm with some people here to do business with your lot. There's a lot of money at stake. I'd hate to have to ruin it now before it even gets a chance to go ahead."

"We are proud people. When we are wronged, then we lose face. If we lose face, then we must correct the problem."

I glanced around me, looking for anyone who might be able to help me out. However, these guys had chosen their place to perfection. It was a narrow alley. No one in sight at all. Which kind of worked in my favor as well.

There were five of them. Too many to fight. Which left me one option. I gave it one last try. "You realize that if something happens to me, and my friends find out then the whole business deal is off?"

The taller Asian man said, "There will be no problem. They won't find you."

"Just so we're clear, you're going to go ahead with this, correct?"

The man nodded and as he did so, the rest drew knives. All except for Broken Jaw who just stood back and waited for the bloodletting to begin.

I gave him a solemn nod and said, "I'm sorry."

"Sorry for what?"

"Sorry that I have to kill you."

My handgun came up and blasted twice, both rounds taking the taller man in the chest. I never waited to see the results as he fell backward before I changed my aim and shot the next man. Again, two more bullets punched into his chest.

Keeping calm, I worked methodically until everyone was down except for the man with a broken jaw. I could see the fear in his eyes and his body was trembling. A wet patch spread at his crotch as my pistol aimed at his head. "This was your fault. It could have been avoided. Now, I guess you'll have to die with the consequences."

I pulled the trigger and his head snapped back, a bloody hole appearing at the center of his forehead. He fell to the ground beside his friends, unmoving.

Quickly glancing around, I looked to see whether anybody was visible or might have witnessed what had gone on. Relieved that the alley was still clear, I placed the handgun back into my waistband.

I left the alleyway and the carnage behind me. But knew that if word of this got out, I would be dead, and it wouldn't be the Asians who killed me.

It would be White.

It was one way of killing the deal, but we still needed to find Crocker.

***

There was no need for concern. Crocker, however, found us. The deal was obviously important enough to pull the man out of hiding. By the time I got back to the hotel, he'd already arrived. As I headed past the reception desk on my way back to my room, one of the clerks called out to me. "Mr. Kane? Mr. Kane?"

I looked around to see a young man waving at me. I changed direction and walked across to the desk. "You called out my name?"

"Yes, sir, you are wanted in the dining room."

"Thank you."

I stood in the doorway which led into the dining area. My eyes scanned the room as I looked for Mr. White. When I saw him, I also saw he was seated with two other men. One was Asian, the other Caucasian. I weaved my way between the diners until I reach their table, White looked up me and said, "Where the hell have you been?"

"I took Jing's advice and became a tourist."

The former general was about to speak but was interrupted by the other man. "Who is this man?"

"Someone I hired the other day. He's good. Saved my life."

"Did you check him out? Is he who he says he is?"

"Of course, I checked him out, and yes, he is who he says he is. John Kane, special forces just got out of Vietnam. He was running missions across the fence."

Suddenly my alarm was going off. The general knew everything about me. But the question was, did he know about the team I took into Cambodia? I guess I'd find out shortly.

The man looked at me. "My name is Crocker. This man over here opposite me is Mr. Ling. We are here discussing business. What I want you to do is sit at the table behind us and see that we're not interrupted."

My mind was whirling. Stuart and I had been convinced that Crocker was in the states, but here he was in Hong Kong. Obviously, the deal was important enough to bring him into the open.

I sat down at the table behind them, scanning the room as I kept an ear peeled to their conversation. I could make out only bits and pieces, not enough. But the main thing was, Crocker was here.

They talked for an hour as they discussed the terms of their deal. They were about to wrap it up when the unexpected happened. An Asian man appeared at the entrance to the dining room, a look of concern on his face. He approached their table and leant down, speaking in a low tone to Ling. The expression on Ling's face began to change, becoming tighter the more he heard from the man.

Then when the informant was done, the mob boss's eyes locked on mine. I knew then that I was in trouble. I heard Mr. White say, "What seems to be the problem?"

"Your man over there, killed some of my men earlier today. He was seen doing it."

Well, that screwed that. Mr. White turned his head and stared at me. "Would you care to explain to me what happened?"

I didn't know what to say. My mind was spinning as I tried to come up with a good enough excuse as to why I'd killed five men. I said, "It was me or them."

My reasoning didn't seem to please Mr. White at all, and when I glanced at Crocker, he looked none too happy either. I waited for them to speak.

To my surprise, it was Crocker who spoke first, he said, "Tell me exactly what happened."

"I went for a walk, had a few drinks, was on the way back to the hotel when these guys appeared in this alley in front of me. I guess they had been watching me. Then they pulled knives on me and like they say back home, don't bring a knife to a gunfight. I gave them several opportunities to leave it alone, that we were here to do business with them, but they were adamant that I had to die."

"Then what happened?"

"What do you think happened? I came back here."

Mr. Ling stared at me. His face remained passive, but his eyes were full of rage. "One of those men was my nephew."

"I'm sorry it was your nephew, but that doesn't change the fact they were trying to kill me."

Crocker said, "The man does have a point, Mr. Ling."

"It's not about points, it's about honor. And right now, honor demands that I kill him."

I was poised for flight. My hand dropped below the table where I was sitting and caressed the butt of the handgun I had on my lap. If it came down to it, it wouldn't take much to bring it up and start shooting. Ling being my first target, Crocker, my second. After that it didn't much matter because the mission would be accomplished.

"I can't let you do that. The man was protecting himself. He doesn't deserve to die for the actions of others."

Ling nodded solemnly before saying, "Then I'm sorry our business is now concluded."

He made to rise before Mr. White stopped him. "Wait. There must be something we can do. There is too much money to be throwing it all in. Everything is already sorted."

"I've already told you what must be done. I can do no more than that."

Mr. White leaned over and whispered something into Crocker's ear. The man's expressions changed a couple of times before he straightened up and said, "Alright, we have a deal."

The surprise was completed when I felt the barrel from Mr. Black's gun stabbing in my side. He said in a low voice, "I'm sorry, old son. But this is business. And you're just a pawn in a much bigger game."

Crocker stared at me. For a moment I thought I saw conflict in his eyes, but it soon disappeared, and he said solemnly, "I'm sorry, Mr. Kane, but business is business and this is worth way too much money for one man to fuck it up."

I felt myself being relieved of my handgun and knew that my window of opportunity had been slammed shut. I nodded. "Guess I'll be seeing you then."

"Somehow I doubt that. If you're ever back State-side, look me up. I've got a job for a man with your talents."

"I'll do that. But if I ever make it back Stateside, you'll be looking for a new place to funnel your drugs through."

He seemed to be amused by this, a smile splitting his face. "I'll give you one thing, Kane; you've got a big pair of balls on you."

"Be seeing you around." I stared at White. "As for you, what happened to no man being left behind, fucking asshole."

He shrugged his broad shoulders. "There is another adage, son. Always look after yourself."

"I'll raise you one. Revenge is a dish best served cold."

I watched them leave and turned my gaze back towards Mr. Ling. "Where do we go from here?"

"I guess you'll have to wait and see."

***

The big man hit me again, this time in the ribs. Pain ripped all through my body as I felt the already cracked rib give way. For two days they'd been working me over, not constantly, just enough to keep me on edge. It was like a slow torture. One eye was swollen almost shut, a tooth was missing, and there were several cuts on my face. Plus, the rib.

When Ling had left, his last words were, keep him alive. So, they did. But that didn't mean they couldn't pound on me some in the meantime.

My hands were tied together above my head, hooked up on a rope which ran up over a rafter. I'd been hanging like this ever since they'd brought me in. At some stage I had pissed myself and I could smell the stench of my sweat as well as the urine.

The door squeaked open just as the man was about to hit me once more. With some effort I raised my head enough to look in that direction. I saw Jing enter. He smiled at me and shook his head. "It look like you not tourist anymore."

"Last piece of fucking advice I take from you," I muttered.

"Too bad, too bad. I think tomorrow they will kill you."

"Thanks for the good news."

As he was such a ray of sunshine, thankfully his visit was brief, and I was soon hanging there again, left to my own devices. The man whose job it was to beat me had left with him, so I went back to work on the bonds above my head. I was almost there. I could feel each strand giving way with the tedious job of plucking at them with a small piece of glass that I had managed to secure upon faking a fall when we'd first arrived. The trick was keeping hold of it. That small shard was all that stood between me and death at that point in time.

As I worked on it, I stared at the window across the room. It was blacked out, but I knew once I got free, it was my ticket out of there. For the next three hours, I worked tirelessly, strand by strand.

I figured on another hour, and I would have been free. Another hour of vigorous sawing at the rope. However, in my exuberance to get freed of my bonds, my fingers had become slippery.

Then I lost the piece of glass. It fell from my grip and hit the floor with a light tinkling sound. I looked down and I saw it bounce away from me. Then it just sat there as though mocking me for my stupidity. I closed my eyes and ground my teeth together as the rage threatened to overwhelm me. But after a few deep breaths, I felt myself relax. All I needed was another plan.

Where the hell was I going to get one of those from?

***

Jing had been right. Mr. Ling came to kill me the following day. He brought with him two other men. I stared at him and said, "No one else? No big fanfare? Just a quiet, peaceful, private ceremony where you get to cut my heart out. I had pictured you as a man who would want something grander."

"Killing you is for my benefit. Nobody else's."

Quick head count. Mr. Ling, Jing, the big bodyguard, and two others. That made five. Not the best of odds, but I'd faced worse in the jungle. And I did have air cover at the time as well, and five or six others to back me up. Still, there are times when one can't pick their battles. This just happened to be one of those. And now the story is caught up.

Ling stepped close to me, his eyes staring hard at my face. I frowned at him. "Is there something wrong? Do I have something of yours on?"

Ignoring my final comment, he said, "I'm staring at your face, so from this day, after you are gone, I can still close my eyes and picture what you looked like just before you died."

"Well, I'm not quite looking my best at the moment. If you let me down, I could tidy up a little for you." It was a poor attempt at humor, but at that point I didn't care.

He held his hand out towards Jing and the little man reached inside his coat and took out a revolver. Why do criminals always have to have revolvers? All those black and white Private Eye movies, all the mob bosses, all the bad guys, always had revolvers. Too bad if you were facing ten men and only had six shots in the wheel.

Mr. Ling took the weapon and raised it at shoulder height. He said, "Do you have any last words, Mr. Kane?"

It sounded like a line out of a James Bond film. I nodded. "How does goodbye feel?"

With all my strength I pulled down. The rope, which was almost cut through, gave way under the pressure I exerted upon it. Stunned by my sudden activity, Ling took a step back. I lurched forward, my hands reaching out. They were still tied, but I managed to grasp the gun that was stuck in his fist. I twisted it violently and his finger snapped in the trigger guard. One of my hands had clamped down upon the hammer making sure that it was immovable, even if he squeezed the trigger.

Ling let out a shriek of pain as I ripped the weapon free. I raised my right foot, kicked him in the stomach, making him stumble backward and fall flat on the floor. I fumbled with the revolver as I managed to turn it around.

The first target was the big man. I owed him and wasn't about to let him get away. The pistol crashed and he staggered under the blow. He dropped to his knees, clutching at the wound.

I thumbed back the hammer and shot the first

of the two bodyguards. He cried out in pain and dropped like the big man did. That left the second guard and Jing, the former being the greatest threat because he had his weapon out.

The gun discharged and I felt the bullet pass close. The man had fired too quickly and missed. I, however, wouldn't make that mistake. The gun barked once more, and the bullet plowed into his chest.

Jing was the last, apart from his boss, but Ling was still on the floor floundering like a fish out of water.

Jing had frozen. The sudden violence from a prisoner had been too much for him, unused to them fighting back. I pointed the revolver at him only to become aware that the adrenaline that had been sustaining me was now wearing off, and the barbs of pain throughout my body were starting to break through.

Out of my good eye, I saw my target and fired. The bullet burned deep into Jing's heart, and he died where he stood.

Turning, I now concentrated all my efforts on Mr. Ling. He was pushing himself away from me on the floor with his hands. "Looks like the shoe is on the other foot now, huh, Mr. Ling?"

His mouth flapped open and closed, but no voice came out. When something eventually did, it was more of a whine than anything else. "Please. Please I can give you money, lots of money."

I glared at him with my one good eye. "I don't want fucking money. You were going to kill me. You had the shit beaten out of me. You expect me to take money for that?"

"Please, please do not do this. I will give you anything."

I shrugged my shoulders. "It's a bit late for that," then I shot him in the head.

***

"Where are you?"

"I'm stuck in Kowloon," I told Stuart.

I went down to give him a rundown of what had happened over the last two days, including the fact that Crocker was in Hong Kong. Surprisingly, Stuart was foremost concerned about my health and Crocker second.

"Listen, get to the embassy. I'll let them know you're coming. They'll get you back to the US."

"Thanks," I replied.

"Tell me about Crocker. Where was he going? Did you hear?"

"As far as I know, they're going back to the US."

"All right, just do as I said. Then I'll see you when you get back."

NEW YORK, 1968...

It was almost two weeks before I arrived back in New York. The people at the embassy decided that I was in no fit condition to fly, so they kept me there under medical watch. By the time I left, my eye had come right down, although it was still bruised, and my rib was mending well. Even the cuts and scrapes were almost healed. And as I found out when I arrived back, a lot had happened. None of it good.

It went like this...

Apparently, after Stuart had finished talking to me, he'd gone to find Clark. He told the CIA man what had happened and asked for assistance monitoring the entry points into New York. It was going to take a lot of manpower, but Clark agreed, and they set up a system.

Two days after I'd finished talking to Stuart, Mr. White arrived via plane back in New York. Together with Mr. Gray and Mr. Black they were ferried from the airport to a different hotel in the city.

Stuart set up a surveillance system with three other agents. But somewhere along the way, one of them had been made and taken off the street.

"Where the hell is he?" Stuart asked a tall man named Brooks.

Brooks shrugged his shoulders. "I have no idea; he just disappeared. I went to take over from him and he was gone."

"Which means we could be compromised."

"Yes, sir."

He looked at Mary. "What do you think?"

"Honestly, I think we're screwed."

Stuart nodded. "See if anything turns up. Even if it's a body, we have to know. In the meantime, we still need to know where Crocker is. Kane said he's coming back here. We need to find out how and where he's entering the country."

"What are you going to do?" Mary asked.

"I think it's time I had a word with our Mr. White."

"Do you think that's wise?" Mary asked.

"We decided to rattle his tree. Let's rattle it a little harder."

***

"Do I know you?" White asked, looking up at Stuart.

Stuart pulled out the chair on the opposite side of the small dining table and sat down. "No, but I know you. General Harold Rivers."

"It would seem you have me at a disadvantage."

Stuart smiled. "Always the first time for everything. Tell me, how's the drug business going?"

The man known as Mr. White froze, a forkful of food halfway to his mouth. He placed the fork back on the plate and then wiped his mouth with a napkin. "Mister, if I was you, I would choose very carefully the next words that came out of my mouth."

But Stuart wasn't thinking. "Tell me how's the drug business coming out of Cambodia these days? Oops. Not really good if I remember rightly."

"Who are you? CIA?"

"I'm the man who's going to shut down your business for good. And you can tell Crocker I'm coming after him next."

Even though he seemed calm on the outside, Rivers's eyes gave away how he was really feeling within. "I'm sorry, son. I don't really know what you're talking about."

Stuart wasn't finished. "Before I go, there was one more thing."

"What was that?"

"You need to find a new pipeline. Mr. Ling had a sudden engagement with an undertaker."

Stuart turned and left after that, leaving a seething Mr. White behind him. The former general looked across at the table next to him, where Mr. Gray and Mr. Black sat. "Follow him. I want to know who he is."

The two men rose from their seats, dropped their napkins on their plates, and started to walk out of the room. White watched them go, his mind still reeling from everything that he'd just heard. If what the man had said was true, and Mr. Ling were dead, then their transportation into the country was dead along with him. And that would cost them a lot of money. If so, someone would pay for it.

Stuart on the other hand had been that wrapped

up in his own little world, running high on the recent confrontation that he became careless. Instead of being cautious and aware of his surroundings, his thoughts were consumed with what else he could have said to Mr. White in the restaurant of the hotel. He failed to notice that he had a tail, and Mr. Gray and Mr. Black were able to follow him without any problem.

When I arrived back in the U.S. Stuart had disappeared and no one knew where he'd got to.

***

I still hurt, just not as much. And I was surprised to see that it was Mary who picked me up from JFK airport. "Where's Cal?" I asked as she pulled away from the pickup zone.

She was quiet.

"Mary?"

"I wish you wouldn't call me Mary," she shot back at me.

"OK, Alice, where is Cal?"

Another drawn-out silence before, "We don't know."

"What do you mean you don't know?"

"That's just it. He's disappeared. We have no idea where Cal is."

She went on to tell me about him meeting with White. And that afterwards he'd called to say that he was going to see Clark, but he never arrived. "We can only assume that he was picked up by the general's men."

"Why the hell would he go and do that alone? He knew it was dangerous."

"The question is what do we do now?" Alice asked me.

"We find him and hope to hell that he's still alive."

We went directly from the airport to see Clark. He was in the same boat we were. There were whispers about, but nothing concrete. "I've had my ear to the ground, Kane, but we can't find out anything. There's no doubt that either the general or Crocker have him, but we don't know where. It's a big city."

"I'm going to need a gun and ammunition. Get me a 1911 if you can."

"What are you going to do?"

"I'm going to find Cal."

Clark nodded. "Get back to your hotel. Give me a bit of time. I'll have a weapon for you and, I'm hoping, a little bit more information. Alice can go with you. She can make sure you don't do anything stupid."

I stared at him. "I don't do stupid, I just do."

***

This time around for Alice and me it was different. Maybe it was because I was developing feelings for her but sleeping with her felt like it meant something. She propped herself up, resting her head on the palm of her hand. "What was that about?"

"What was what about?" I asked.

"You know what I'm talking about. The last time we slept together it wasn't like that."

"Maybe this time it was different," I told her.

"I'll say it was damn different."

Suddenly I felt uncomfortable and started to get up. However, Alice stopped me with a hand on my arm. "Don't go. I'm sorry."

I sat on the edge of the bed staring at the large, curtained window. There was movement behind me as Alice repositioned herself on the bed. Her arms wrapped around me, and I felt her breasts press against my back. She said in a soft voice, "Did you feel it too, John?"

I nodded slowly. "Yes, I think so."

"What do we do about it?" she asked.

"I don't know."

Her hands parted and she ran her fingers over the bruises on my back. "Do they hurt?"

"A little bit," I allowed.

"Please lay down."

I did as she asked and then she lay beside me with her head on my chest. Well, I liked that for the next hour we talked about everything. I guess it was a way of forgetting about our predicament. And then after that we made love again.

It wasn't until mid-morning the following day that Clark got back to me, and the news wasn't good.

"We can confirm that White or Rivers, however you want to call him, has Cal," he told me as he sat down on the chair.

"How did you confirm it?"

"They sent us proof."

"What sort of proof?"

"You don't need to know. The issue is finding out where they are holding him."

"What do they want?"

"Nothing."

I didn't understand. "How could they not want anything?"

"Because they're going to kill him," Alice said. "Aren't they? They're going to make an example of him."

Clark nodded. "That's what we assume."

"Do you have any idea where he is? Or even they are?"

With a shake of his head, Clark answered. "None at all."

"Then we need to find someone who does. What about family? Does Rivers have any?"

"He has an ex-wife who lives in Middletown. She might know something, but I don't know."

"Get me an address," I said. "It's worth a try. Anything is worth a try now."

**

Clark found me a car. It was a blue 1968 Pontiac Firebird. And it ran like a dream. Alice came with me up to Middletown. I figured it was better to have a female along to put Mrs. Rivers's mind at ease. We arrived late in the afternoon just as the sun was starting to sink, forming a dappled pattern across the road which led up to the house surrounded by a small forest.

I eased the Pontiac to a stop and then waited, staring silently at the house before us. It was a longshot, but at that moment it was all we had. Meanwhile, Clark had his people working on trying to dig up anything they could find. That, however, was proving difficult because Crocker knew all the tricks and he used them to his advantage.

The screen door on the house opened and a thin woman with graying hair and wearing a blue dress emerged. Alice and I climbed out of the Pontiac and walked towards the steps leading up onto the porch. Our shoes crunched on the gravel drive.

"Who are you?" she called to us, her voice dry and raspy, sounding as though she smoked more than a pack a day.

"Are you Mrs. Rivers?" I called back.

"Not anymore, I'm not."

At least we had the right place. "Mrs. Rivers, we're from the government. We'd like to talk to you if we may?"

"I've got nothing to say to you. Don't come any closer." Her voice was quite firm. "Just get back in your fancy car and leave."

"It's very important that we talk to you, Mrs. Rivers," Alice said. "You may not be able to help us, but you might."

"What about?"

"Your former husband."

She sighed, relenting easily. "You'd better come in."

We climbed the stairs and followed her inside. When we reached the living room, she said, "I didn't catch your names."

"Mary and Paul," Alice lied.

"I'll take it that those aren't your real names, but they'll do. My name is Gwen."

"Pleased to meet you, ma'am," I said.

"Can I get you anything?"

"No, thank you," Alice replied.

"You'd better tell me what he's done now," Gwen sighed. "Although, if I had to guess it would be bad to have the CIA knocking on my door."

Alice said, "Do you know of a man called Mason Crocker?"

Gwen frowned thoughtfully. "I don't think I have."

"Nothing at all?"

With a shake of her head she said, "No. What is this about?"

"We can't exactly tell you that, Gwen."

She flipped her hands in the air helplessly. "Of course, you can't. I don't even know why you bothered coming here. I haven't seen him in three years."

"Is there somewhere your former husband might go to get away from everything? Somewhere he might go to ground?" I asked her.

"He used to go to our cabin a lot, but since we divorced it's been unused. I was thinking about selling it."

"Could you show me on a map where it is?"

"Sure. I think I have one here somewhere."

She disappeared from the room and Alice said, "You figure they're hiding out until things cool off?"

"Might be an idea. Or they're laying low so they can get out of the country."

"And go where?"

"Back to Vietnam."

"Here it is," Gwen said as she entered the room holding the unfolded map.

She laid it out on a small coffee table, and we had a look at it. She stabbed at it with a crooked finger and said, "Up here, in the Adirondacks."

The area to which she pointed looked reasonably secluded. All the better for hiding out. I looked at Alice and said, "Looks like as good a place as any."

"I guess it could be a good place to start. Considering we haven't got anything else to go on."

I looked at Gwen and said, "Thank you. We really

appreciate your help. I'm sorry to have troubled you."

"Be careful; he's a very dangerous man. I ought to know. I was married to him for fifteen years."

We left the home in the woods and headed back towards town. Alice said to me, "Are we headed up there now?"

"Not yet, I need to get a few things."

She looked confused. "What do you mean you?"

"The cabin is in the mountains in the middle of nowhere. Surrounded by thick forest. This is what I do. This is my job. I go in alone."

***

"Are you sure you want to do this?" Clark asked me when we returned.

"Yes, like I told Alice, it's what I do. I can get in there, look around and get out. They won't even know I'm there. If they are even there," I replied.

"What will you need?"

I thought for a moment before answering. "A CAR-15, ammunition, a handgun, black face paint, and a knife."

Clark nodded. "I think we can do all that. Is there anything else you need?"

"Insertion. If you can get me a helicopter to get me up there somewhere, I'll do the rest."

"We're the CIA, we can do anything," Clark said grimly. "But if you find Cal, you need to get him out."

The only way I would be able to do that is to take down everyone I found on site. "You know what that means, don't you?"

"I do. Whatever it takes, if he's there, you get him out."

"If he's there, I'll get him."

Clark was about to leave when I thought of something else I might need. "Get me a couple of grenades. They might come in handy."

"If I can get my hands on them, you'll have them."

He left the room to make a phone call, leaving me and Alice on our own. She walked over beside me and said, "Are you sure you're up to this, John?"

I looked into her eyes, and I could see the tenderness and concern there. Suddenly I felt something that I hadn't felt in a long time. I took her into my arms and said, "I'll be fine. It's what I do, remember?"

"But you'll be on your own and there will be so many of them."

"Nothing I'm not used to."

We stood there holding each other for a long time until Alice stepped back and looked into my eyes once more. "What is it?" I asked.

She hesitated for a moment before saying, "When this is over, John, I want to be with you."

I frowned. "What do you mean?"

"I want us to be together."

I stared at her for a moment, processing what she had just said. There was nothing that I wanted more at that moment. However, I found myself saying, "I don't know if that's possible, Alice. For all I know, I'll be sent back to Vietnam. You'll be going back to your work with the CIA?"

"But you won't be in Vietnam forever, John. What about when you come back, return home? What then?"

"I don't know. I'll have to go where they post me."

There was desperation in her eyes. "But we can try, can't we? We can at least try."

"All right. How about we talk it over some more once we're done here?"

Panic flared in her eyes, but she pushed it aside. "You're not trying to fob me off, are you, John?"

I shook my head. "No, I promise I'm not, I promise you. We will talk about this again. And I can tell you right now there's nothing I want more than to be with you."

She lifted her head up and kissed me on the lips. I felt a tingle run the length of my body. I knew then that I would do everything I could to make it work with her. This was a woman that one day I would marry.

The door to the room opened, and Clark returned. "I can get you everything you need, Kane. When do you want to go?"

I looked at my watch. It was mid-morning. "How about later this afternoon? If I can arrive at the LZ just before dark, it'll suit me fine."

"Consider it done."

ADIRONDACK MOUNTAINS, 1968...

I felt at home. The dark, the thick trees. It felt good. I'd been inserted two hours before, now I was sitting on my own in the darkness waiting. The helicopter had dropped me four miles from the cabin, and I'd covered 3 miles before I settled down for the evening. I'd stay in position until the early hours and maybe break camp about three.

The night gave me a lot of time to reflect. Thinking about Vietnam. About all the friends I'd lost and how this would go some way to bring redemption.

I dozed on and off until the time came where I got up off the damp ground and stretched out the kinks.

It took me almost an hour to cover the rest of the distance to where I set up a position overlooking the cabin and waited. The building itself was surrounded by a thick stand of trees. But I could see the smoke rising from the chimney on top of the roof. Someone was there.

In the east, dawn was dying as the sun slowly began coming up over the mountains, filtering through the forest and causing a dappled pattern over the earth below the canopy. In it, I could see the guards at their posts. It was time to go to work.

I slipped from behind a large granite boulder and down a gentle slope. I circled around to the left towards the first guard who was positioned at the rear of the cabin. I reached a point where I lay the CAR-15 down and drew my knife.

Using all the stealth I had at my disposal, I slipped up behind him and clamped my left hand over his mouth. In my right hand, the knife that I held plunged downward into his chest twice before I drew the blade across his throat.

I lowered him gently to the ground and then glanced around to make sure that I hadn't been seen. I hurriedly covered him with leaf litter before I retrieved the CAR-15 and slipped back into the woods to creep up on the second guard.

Getting rid of guards two and three went pretty much to plan. Using a number of the skills in my repertoire, I dispatched them with ease and brutal force.

I scouted the area around the cabins some more and found the last guard in amongst some rocks to the east. I almost missed him, but the cigarette smoke gave his position away. If we'd been in the jungle in Vietnam and one of my men had done that, I'd have kicked them off the team for putting us all in danger.

The guard was tired, lazy. It was easy to creep up behind him, place the sharp edge of the blade of my knife at his throat and say, "Make a sound and I'll open you up from ear to ear."

The man stiffened as the point of the blade just pricked the skin enough to draw blood. With my point made, I whispered in his ear, "How many in the cabin?"

At first, he said nothing, so I asked the question again. "How many in the cabin?"

"There are three."

"Who?"

"The general, Travis, and Bolton."

"What about Crocker?" I hissed

"He's not here."

"Where is he?"

"I don't know."

"What about the CIA agent you picked up?"

"He—he's not here either."

"Where is he?"

"At another location. The general is going there today."

"What for?" I asked.

The man never spoke.

"What for?" This time I spoke more forcefully.

"To get rid of him," the man replied weakly.

I processed the news for a moment and then asked, "Do you have any family?"

"No."

"Too bad," I said, and cut his throat anyway.

I put my knife away and then took the CAR-15, making sure I had a round in the breech. Approaching the cabin, keeping to the side where there were no windows. I could hear voices inside as I moved furtively around the exterior of the building. I stepped up onto the porch and moved closer to the front door, careful to stay under the window height.

When I reached the door, I took a deep breath before taking the handle in my hand. I slowly turned it until the door slipped ajar. Then, taking another breath I entered the cabin.

All three men were standing in the centre of

the room. Rivers and Travis and Bolton. Known as
Mr. Black and Mr. Gray. Travis moved first, but my
weapon came around and I sprayed him with a short
burst of fire. He cried out in pain and fell to the floor,
a ghastly wound in his chest.

Then my aim turned to Bolton, who already had
his handgun out and was about to fire. The CAR-
15 roared again and soon the former CIA man lay
beside his friend.

Now I turned my concentration to the former
general. "Told you I would be back, General."

"You're certainly resilient, son. I'll give you that."

"I guess you have to be in my line of work."

"Is that working for the CIA?"

"Amongst other things," I allowed.

"You certainly had me fooled, son," he said. "Was
it you who killed Mr. Ling?"

I nodded. "It was him or me; I decided that him
was better."

"So where does that leave us?"

"Where's Cal?" I asked him.

"Oh, yes, our friend from the CIA," Rivers
sneered.

"Where is he?" I asked again.

"I don't know."

The lie rankled, so I shot him. Not in the chest or
anywhere fatal, but in the leg, somewhere that's nice
and meaty and hurts a lot. He went down in a heap
on the floor, a hole in his leg the size of an acorn.
Blood began flowing freely, forming a pool on the
wooden floor. I stepped closer to him and put my
foot on the wound. He cried out in pain.

"Let's try again, shall we? Where is Cal?"

"You know," Rivers grated through clenched

teeth, "you could always come back and work for us."

I shook my head slowly and put more pressure on the wound. "Where?"

"All right, all right. He's ten miles from here at an old farmhouse east of Copperville. You'll find him easy enough. Has the name of Morris on the mailbox."

"Tell me the address."

Between gasping in pain and taking in big breaths, Rivers eventually got it out. I stepped back off the leg and stood there in silence, staring at his pathetic form in front of me. He looked back up at me. His face was now bathed in sweat.

"Where's Crocker?"

This question drew a different response as Rivers snorted with derision. "You don't think I'm going to tell you that, do you? If you do, you're one dumb sonofabitch."

I contemplated standing back on the wound again, then decided against it. Instead, I shot him a second time, the discharge of the weapon loud within the confines of the cabin. The former general howled in pain as the bullet punched through his leg and into the floorboards beneath him. This time when I spoke, my voice was harsh. "I've got plenty of fucking bullets left. Make a choice. I can do this all day."

To my surprise he chuckled through the pain. "What's so funny?"

"You. This is bigger than you. Even bigger than me or Crocker."

"What do you mean?"

"It takes a lot of money to set this kind of thing

up. Where do you think it comes from?"

"I have no idea."

A spark of hope glimmered in his eyes. "I'll give you a name."

"What do you want in return?" I asked him.

"Let me go. Just walk away."

I grinned at him, my teeth showing extra white against my dark face. "If I find Crocker, I'll get it from him."

I raised my weapon to shoot him. The general's hand flew up. "Stop!"

"Why?"

"Because you don't know what you're getting yourself into," he blurted out. "The man in charge is very powerful."

"What is he? Government official? A senator?"

Rivers shook his head. "No, he's more powerful than that."

"How can he be more powerful than that?"

"He's part of a conglomerate. They use all the money they get from the drugs to strengthen their position. They're like a government behind the government. They have influence, power. They decide what decisions the government makes."

I didn't know whether to believe him or not. The story sounded a little far-fetched. "So you're saying Crocker isn't the man in charge?"

"He's the man in charge of the drug operation. But not the man in charge of everything else."

"What do they call themselves?" I asked.

"They don't call themselves anything. That way, no one knows they even exist."

I still wasn't convinced. "How do they influence the government?"

"Through donations. They are the biggest donors to government officials in the country. If the officials don't do what they want, their funds are withheld. And in this country, with this government, money is power. Only in this case, all to the wrong people."

"Give me a name."

"If I do, you have to walk away," Rivers said. "I'll be as good as dead anyway, but this way I'll have a chance."

I thought about it for a moment. Then I asked him one burning question, "Who is in charge in Vietnam and Cambodia?"

"Bob Little, why?"

"Is he the Marine?"

"He was."

I thought for a moment, and something came to me. The CIA man that I had pegged in Mama San's bar. If I was a betting man, that was Crocker.

"Was he the one that gave the order to wipe out my team? Or Crocker?"

Rivers frowned. "Wait, were you there? Were you part of what happened in Vietnam? And in Cambodia."

"I lost nearly every man in my team," I snarled at him. "Remember this name as you burn in hell. ST Denver."

Then I shot him.

***

I found the mailbox on the gravel road and turned off onto the long driveway. I'd taken the Thunderbird that Rivers had been using; after all, he wouldn't be needing it.

The vehicle rolled to a stop, and I climbed out

carrying my automatic rifle. But surprisingly, there was no one there, which troubled me even more. I walked up to the base of the steps and looked at the front door of the house. It was slightly ajar.

Slowly I climbed the stairs and onto the porch, crossing cautiously to the doorway. I gently pushed the door open, and it squeaked on its hinges. I waited momentarily for something to happen, but it never did.

Crossing the threshold, I started a thorough check of each room as I came across them. Each time I found them empty. By the time I had reached the rear of the house, there was nothing to find.

I walked to the back door and looked out through the large pane in the top of it. It was then that I noticed something. My blood ran cold as I opened the door. By the time I reached the yard, I had a bad feeling. A really bad feeling. I stopped and looked down at the mound of dirt at my feet. Lengthwise, it would have covered a man. And I remembered Rivers's words. "You can't miss it."

On hands and knees, I started scraping the dirt away. Eventually I uncovered some fabric from an article of clothing. I moved to a new area and slowly scraped the soil away until I had revealed a face. I leaned back on my knees and muttered a curse. I was too late. The bastards had already killed Cal.

THE PRESENT...

Kane read the line four times before he was convinced of what it had said. Cal Stuart died in 1968. If that was true, then who was the old man that he'd spent hours with who'd encouraged him to keep reading the diary.

Something was dreadfully amiss, and Kane needed answers. Here he was in Vietnam with people he thought he knew—and there it was. The people he thought he knew weren't who they said they were. They couldn't be. So what was their game? More importantly, who could he trust?

Sara appeared. "Is everything all right?"

His head whipped up. "Yes, fine."

"How is it going with the diary. Anything interesting?"

"It's all interesting."

"Sorry, not what I meant. Is there any information that we can use now that we've lost Cal?"

"Nothing yet," Kane replied.

She nodded. "All right, I'll check in again later."

Kane went back to the diary and Sara left him to it. Outside, Peters was waiting for her and he asked, "Well?"

"I think he knows something."

"Shit," Peters hissed. "What do we do?"

"Put the others on standby just in case. The boss will be here soon then it will all be over."

"I hope you're right."

SOUTH VIETNAM, 1968...

I was back where I started. In the suffocating heat and bug infestations of South Vietnam. It was Hollister that picked me up from the plane. And he took me to a secluded location where he could ask me questions without interruption.

"Do you want to tell me what happened back in the states?" the MP general asked.

I filled him in on what had happened right up to the point where I'd shot Rivers and found Stuart's body. "They just shot him in the head and buried him. Like a dog."

"And he said Crocker was back in Vietnam."

"That's what he said."

"The problem is going to be finding him," Hollister said thoughtfully.

I already had a plan for that. "When you shut the operation down, this end, did you get a guy called Bob Little, former Marine captain?"

Hollister shook his head. "I can't say we did. There were a few that we missed, but their operation is screwed. Do you think he can help you find Crocker?"

"I know he can."

"What's that other part about a conglomeration or some bullshit? You know, the thing about the businessmen, the donors to the government."

"Rivers said that's where they were getting all their money from. The men behind the scenes were financing them so they could manufacture the drugs, take them back, sell them, and make a huge profit. Then they use that money as donations for members of the government. The bigger the donation, the more pull they have. Rivers described it as a government behind the government."

"It sounds like some conspiracy theory out of a damn book."

"That's why we need to find out if it's true or not," I told him.

"So where are you going to look?"

"A place called Mama San's."

***

"Hey, Joe, you're back," the prostitute said with more than a glint in her eye. "You want fuck?"

I shook my head. "Not tonight."

She looked disappointed. "Why not? I not see you long time. Where you been?"

"On leave."

"You want drink instead?"

"Yeah, give me a beer." I put some money on the table for her to take. "I want the change."

She gave me an indignant look. "Do you think I thief?"

I grinned at her. "I didn't say that."

"Asshole."

She returned with my drink a couple of minutes

later, placed it on the table in front of me. Before she left, she winked at me and said, "If you want me, you know where I am? Plenty ready for you."

I sat there for the next half hour, watching people come and go. Most were soldiers.

Just when I was about to give up for the night, he appeared, flanked by two other men.

He looked around Mama San's and spotted me. My hand was under the table gripping the 1911 as he approached.

"So, you're back. Not a wise move on your part."

"You made a wise move, Little," I shot back at him.

He frowned, puzzled that I knew who he was. "You brought two goons with you. It's a pity they're frigging useless."

His eyes widened as the weapon came clear of the table. The 1911 fired twice and both the man's friends dropped to the floor and never moved. I changed my aim but never fired. His hands flew up to shoulder height as he cried out, "Don't shoot!"

Shouts of alarm sounded through the club as panic set in. Three armed men came out of their seats and said above the noise, "MPs! Everybody, calm down."

They walked over to the table where I still had Little under my gun. His expression changed once he realized what was happening. "You rotten son of a bitch."

I climbed to my feet and said, "It's time you answered some questions, Little. It's in your best interest that you do, because..." I shrugged. "Well, just because."

"I'll damned well tell you nothing," he snarled.

"Yes, you will. Of that, I'm quite confident."

***

They all crack in the end. I won't go into details about how we extracted the information but let's just say that tough guy Little wasn't so tough after all.

"There's a village in Laos. About six miles across the border. After the Cambodia operation was shut down, Crocker moved it there."

"I can't understand how he can operate in the middle of a war zone," I said.

"Money. You pay the right people, and you never have to worry."

"I want you to show me on a map exactly where it is."

After he had done so, I looked at Hollister. "Looks like I've got another mission to run."

"You'll need a good team."

"I'll take the same team I took last time."

"Alright, I'll get you right up to MACV SOG."

"Thanks."

***

I was sent up to FOB 1 (Forward Operating Base 1) at Phu Bai where I was to meet up with the others. When I arrived, I found out different. Chuck Wallis wasn't there. Neither were his Yards.

I found out from Dick Reynolds that a week before, ST Waco had been ambushed running a mission into Laos. According to Dick, the insertion had gone to plan. But later that evening, just before dark, they ran into a NVA tracker team with dogs.

The team had pushed through the night trying to break free of their pursuers until morning so they could call in an evac. Just after dawn, Covey received his radio message that the team was still being pursued. But they were hopeful that they could reach the LZ before the NVA caught up to them. However, it was hammer and anvil tactics.

The pursuers drove the SOG team straight into a larger, company size, NVA force. They didn't even know they were there until they opened fire cutting down Wallis's one-one in the first fusillade.

The team formed up in a wagon wheel formation, each man watching his front. Wallis' one-two, and radio operator, Henry Saville had been in touch with Covey throughout the initial contact.

Had reported that two Yards had gone down along with the one-one. Wallis was wounded as he tried to bring his man back in, but it was futile. So instead, the team hunkered down in the staggered wagon wheel.

When I asked how many men had gone in, I was told eight, which was a heavy team.

Covey had called air support, but by the time it arrived, all contact had been lost with the ground.

Later that day, a hatchet force was spun up. It was led by Dick Reynolds. When they were first inserted, they found nothing. Just spent casings and flattened areas where the battle had been fought. However, after an hour of searching, they found the first body. It had been stripped and dismembered. Further investigation ascertained that it was the radio operator, Henry Saville. They never found anyone else.

I looked at Dick Reynolds, shook my head upon hearing the news. "That's just fucked up."

The SOG man nodded.

"What about your team, Dick?" I asked.

"They're on leave. I got pulled out of a bar to come up here."

"Then we'll have to pull something together. Are there many operators here at the minute?"

"There are three Recon teams out in the field. But there might be a few people here willing to go out for a run."

"One more SF man and two Yards should do the job," I told him.

"Let's go and find them then."

Five minutes later, we were talking to a shirtless guy wearing sunglasses, sitting on a sandbag wall. "Tommy 'Shockwave' Power," I said recognising him immediately.

He swung his legs over the wall and sat upright. "Reaper, is that you?"

"You know it is, Shockwave."

"Thank Christ for that. I was beginning to think that beer from last night was still blurring my vision."

"What are you doing here? Why aren't you out?"

"Herman's out there. Breaking in a new guy, didn't want to go in one extra heavy."

I stared at him knowing that what he said wasn't quite the truth. "You want to try that again?"

"Fair enough, I was still drunk this morning when they went out. We weren't on the roster, but all of a sudden shit happened out in the Boondocks and we were spun up. There was no way I could go. So Herman went one light."

"Not ideal, Shockwave," I said. When a team was out in the jungle, even with one light it could compromise the whole system.

Shockwave nodded. "I know, Reaper, you don't have to lecture me."

"How are you feeling now?" I asked him.

"Hell, I'm fine now."

"Dick and I are looking for a one-two, you up for it?"

Shockwave came to his feet and stood to attention. "I'm as ready as I'll ever be. I'm in."

"Good, all I need now is a couple of Montagnards."

"I saw Jimmy getting around two the other day. He's been strapping for different teams when they need an extra person," Shockwave explained.

"Do you think you can find him?" I asked.

"Sure, I can."

"Then get to it."

Shockwave walked off and I turned around to Dick Reynolds. "One more Yard will do it."

"You haven't exactly told me what your plan is," he said.

"Prisoner snatch."

He was confused. "What kind of prisoner?"

A few minutes later, he knew everything that I did.

"That's it? We just go in there and grab our man and get out."

"That's it," I said.

"That's a lot of trouble just for one man, Reaper."

"It is, but he's the key to stopping this."

"I sure hope you're right," Reynolds said.

"So do I."

Here we were again. It seemed like things had come full circle. We were making our way through the jungle with torturously slow precision. The team had been inserted the evening before, just before dark on our secondary LZ. As soon as we had taken off, I decided to scrap the primary just in case the mission had been compromised. You never could be too careful. Dick Reynolds was in agreement with my choice and the change in plan had been relayed to Covey.

We spent the night under triple canopy in the lee of a large mountain. Everything was unusually quiet, but I wasn't one to complain. Following morning we were up early and traversing the country towards our target. Around midmorning we crossed a stream with steep embankments on either side. It was slow flowing, so it wasn't too bad to get across, even though both sides were muddy and slippery.

Once across it, we climbed slowly until we topped a ridge before working our way down the other side. It was mid-afternoon when we reached the village.

We found a good place for an OP and then settled in to watch over the village and come up with a plan to get Crocker. If he was there.

A further hour and we were able to ascertain he was indeed there. Then we waited for dark.

After the sun had gone down, Reynolds and I slipped into the village. The huts were elevated off the ground, so we were able to use them to our advantage, keeping to the shadows. We were soon towards the center of the village. And closer to the hut where Crocker had set up as his base.

However, we did have to be careful because there were guards who walked the perimeter and patrolled through the village. At one stage I was about the duck out from underneath the hut when Dick grabbed my shoulder and held me back.

Once the threat passed, we crossed the open area and underneath a different hut where we could get a good look at our target building. Dick's voice got close to my ear, and he whispered, "How do you want to do this?"

From where I hid, I looked at the hut where Crocker was. The light was on inside and shone out through the window.

We waited patiently for the next ten minutes as we timed the passage of the guards. Once we were confident enough, I slithered out from underneath the hut where we were hiding.

Reynolds followed me and soon we were crouched at the bottom of the stairs leading up into Crocker's hut.

As I put my foot on the first step, Reynolds remained at the bottom with his CAR-15 watching for anyone coming past. Once I reached the top, he followed me up.

I pushed the door open and stepped swiftly through, surprising Crocker who was sitting on a chair near a table. "Make a noise and I'll put a bullet in your head," I hissed.

"Well, well. You tell a man to look you up and here he is. I gather Rivers told you where I was. Either that or Little. I'm guessing Little."

"Both," I told him.

He nodded. "So where do we go from here, gents?"

Not moving my carbine, I said to Reynolds, "Get him ready to go."

"Are we going somewhere?"

"We are. You've got a lot of questions to answer, Crocker."

Within a few minutes, he was ready to travel, hands tied behind his back and a gag over his mouth. I said to Reynolds as I drew my knife, "Lead us out."

My plan was that if Crocker tried to raise the alarm, I'd use my knife and cut his throat. That way, without gunfire we wouldn't draw too many people.

I closed the door behind us as we went down the stairs. We crossed over the narrow gap, then in under the hut opposite. Suddenly Dick stopped us.

Even though I couldn't see his hand signals, I knew there was something wrong. Most likely a guard. He tapped me once on the shoulder to make sure I remained in place with our prisoner.

He slipped out from under the hut. Stood up, then closed the gap between himself and the guard. Only a matter of metres.

There was a faint grunt as Reynolds plunged the knife into the man's chest and then finished him off by opening his throat. He dragged the guard in under the hut where Crocker and I were hiding, the smell of coppery blood heavy in the air.

Once the way was clear, we kept moving using the shadows. Finally, we reached the tree line at the edge of the village. Luck had gone our way.

Once in the jungle, I began to relax a little; not much. Just a little.

We hunched down together in the jungle. I said to Shockwave, "See if you can raise Covey. Tell them we're good to go, will need King Bees at the LZ in the morning."

I had arranged for a night flight. Just to make sure someone was up in case anything went wrong with the infiltration into the camp.

A few minutes later, Shockwave got back to me. "We're good to go, Reaper. The King Bees will be there in the morning, so will Covey."

"Then I guess all we have to do now is make it to the LZ in one piece." I called Jimmy over. "You lead; get us out of here."

"Sure thing, boss," he replied and disappeared into the jungle.

SOUTH VIETNAM, 1968...

"There is nothing more I'd like to do now than put a bullet in your fucking brain," I said to Crocker, who sat cuffed to the chair.

The former CIA man smiled confidently. "I'm guessing I'm alive for a reason. How about you tell me what it is?"

"Tell us about the conglomerate. The people who are driving the government from the shadows."

He raised an eyebrow. "Wow. You finally realized this is bigger than you."

"Just answer the fucking question, asshole," Hollister growled.

"What happened to Rivers?"

I didn't lie. "He's dead, I killed him. But not before he talked about the conglomerate. However, he didn't give me a name."

Crocker nodded knowingly. "So that's why I'm still alive."

"I can't think of any other reason."

"Straightforward and honest. All the qualities I like in a man."

"Are you going to give me a name or not?"

Crocker sighed. "You know what, I think I will. I just hope you know what you're getting yourself in for."

"Just like that?" I said.

He nodded. "Yes, this ought to be interesting."

"Well?"

"His name is Ralph Palmer. He's the man behind the biggest real estate boom in American history. New towns springing up across the country and he's behind the lot of them."

"Never heard of him. What about you, General?"

Hollister nodded slowly. "I've heard of him. Palmer Enterprises. There's a new town in Michigan just down the road from where I live that is starting to go up. My wife is saying it's just growing overnight."

Crocker grinned. "And how do you think he's getting the go ahead for all of these projects? Donations. Millions of dollars into the right pocket and there you go. It's the same with the oil industry in Texas. Two years ago, a new oilfield was discovered. But they're sitting on it. It's capable of producing a million barrels a day. However, they are just waiting for the right time to start it."

"Who's in charge of that?" I asked.

"Teddy Sanford, the biggest oil baron in Texas."

"How can they sit on that much oil and it not get out?"

"Money," Crocker said. "It's all about money."

I glanced at Hollister, who already had a troubled expression on his face. "And these guys run the government from behind the scenes?"

Crocker shook his head. "No, there's more of

them. Ed Randall, the supermarket giant. Taffy Smith, the mining billionaire. Archibald Lester, shipping tycoon out of Louisiana. Everything to do with trade, infrastructure etc, etc."

"Now they've turned drug dealers?" I asked Crocker.

"It's not about the drugs, it's about the money. Don't you understand that yet? The more they earn, the more they can donate, or grease wheels if you like, and the more they can control."

I frowned. "Surely no one can control a whole government."

It was the general that set me straight. "They don't have to control the whole government. All they need to do is control votes. If they can do that, then they can get anything knocked back or passed that they see fit. Hence controlling all of the policy that passes through it."

"All right, but what if they don't want to play along?"

Crocker stared at me. "Two words, Kane. Senator Bowman."

I looked at Hollister. "Who is Senator Bowman?"

Hollister said, "Was, Kane. Who *was* Senator Bowman?"

"Exactly," said Crocker. "Who *was* Senator Bowman?"

"I will bite," I said. "Who was the senator?"

It was Crocker who told me. "Senator Martin Bowman from Kentucky. Last year, when a construction bill was to be passed through the House, which would have benefited Palmer, the bill looked like it would be voted down. They only needed a handful of votes to get it across the line. It was worth millions of dollars to the Palmer Enterprises. Anyhow, poor Senator Martin Bowman was the one picked to make an example of. Official cause of death was a heart attack. But if the body had gone to any other medical examiner than the one that was chosen, they might have found the small needle mark in the back of his neck. Everyone knew that it wasn't a heart attack. And just that alone was enough to get the bill passed."

"So that is how it's done?"

"Basically. It's simplifying it a bit, but yes."

I looked at Hollister. This was way beyond anything I knew how to deal with. "What do we do now?"

"First we put this guy on ice some place where nobody knows where he is. Going to be needed. And he knows that. Secondly, I have to kick this up the chain."

I had a thought. "What about the CIA?"

"What about them?" Hollister asked.

"They have certain ways of dealing with things that go unnoticed. Maybe if I reach out to Clark? Something might be able to be done."

For a moment, it seemed as though Hollister wasn't going to agree. But then an expression came to his face that seemed to me like he was happy to be rid of the problem. "All right. I'll get you a flight back to the States. Take this guy with you. The sooner he's out of my hair, the better."

I nodded in agreement. "Thanks for your help,

General."

"Don't thank me yet. This whole thing is fucked up beyond all recognition."

"Then I guess I'll have to unfuck it."

NEW YORK, 1968...

I delivered Crocker to Clark and spent the next day with Alice waiting for news. We were both called back to Clark's current abode where he filled us in on what he'd learned.

"Crocker gave us quite a lot," he told us. "The working of the drug scene which we passed on to the FBI. And how the conglomerate works."

"I thought government officials were influenced by donations anyway?" I said.

"To some degree they are. What makes this lot different is that they just don't use money. They use blackmail and murder as well. They literally set government policy."

"So, what do we do about it?"

"We stop them," Clark said simplistically.

"How do we do that?"

"We find the weakest link and use it against them."

"And who is the weakest link?" I asked.

"The one with the most to lose."

I thought about it for a moment before saying,

"Ralph Palmer. Everyone will point the finger at him if they're caught, leaving him to take the blame for it all. But if we take him, then he will give us everyone."

Clark grinned. "Sounds like a plan."

"But what if we can't get him?"

"Then he dies."

I had no argument with that.

"Where do we find him?"

"Right here in New York. He is here meeting with the governor about a development in the city. Of course, a hundred thousand dollars goes a long way to grease the wheels."

"We'd better come up with a plan, then."

"Easy," Clark said. "Go to his room, kidnap him, put him in a laundry trolley, and then wheel him out of there."

"Glad to see you've given it some thought," I replied.

"Sometimes the simplest options are always the best. Are you in?"

"I've come this far; I'm staying with the ship until it sinks."

"Let's hope it doesn't."

***

The red and black bellhop uniform I was wearing felt strange. I thought of a performing monkey and figured I had to look close. But at least I had a place for my weapon.

As I crossed the lobby I glanced at the desk where Alice was dealing with a customer. She glanced at me, and I gave her a slight nod.

She said something to the desk clerk beside her before apologizing to the customer and coming out from behind the polished hardwood counter.

She walked towards me as I continued moving towards the bank of elevators. We met up at the first one and she pushed the button which brought the elevator to us. "Nice uniform," she said out of the corner of her mouth.

"Shut up," I shot back in a low voice.

The elevator arrived and we got in. Alice pressed the button for the twentieth floor and the carriage started its climb. "Palmer is in room twenty-thirteen. The room next to it has the trolley in it. He has two other men with him. They'll have to be taken out first."

"Piece of cake," I said with more than a hint of sarcasm.

The bell dinged to let us know we'd arrived on our floor, and we stepped out into a hallway laid with brown carpet. "This way," Alice said to me, and I followed her to the right.

We found the room and Alice knocked on the door while I stood off to one side.

I heard a muffled, 'who is it?' And then Alice said, "It's Mary from the front desk. I have been asked to come up because there were reports of excessive noise coming from this room."

I waited for a few moments before the door opened. Alice had taken a couple of steps back which allowed me a passage in front of her.

As soon as the door opened, I made my move. Stepping forward I jammed the barrel of the 1911 into the man's middle and said in a low voice, "Shout and I'll spill your guts."

He froze and allowed me to reach inside his coat and remove the revolver he had hidden there and give it to Alice. "Turn around and start walking."

When we moved along the short hallway a voice called out, "Get rid of them, Luke."

Entering the room proper, it was the second bodyguard who realized something was wrong. My vision was blocked by the man in front of me which permitted the second guard to get his weapon out. Things went downhill from there.

The second bodyguard fired his weapon at me, the bullet passing close to my head. It punched into the wall behind me, and I ducked reflexively. I came back up, without thinking, and all my military training taking over, I fired back.

The bullet punched into his chest, and he cried out as he fell backwards. I cursed silently under my breath. This was the last thing we needed.

The first bodyguard spun around taking me by surprise. His hand lashed out, catching me on the jaw. I reeled backward, stars flashing in my eyes and a stunned feeling buzzing through my head.

The 1911 fell to the floor at my feet and I tried to dive down to pick it up. But the first bodyguard had other ideas, and he hit me from the side, lunging at me, driving me backward. I staggered and fell with him on top of me, I landed on the coffee table and wood splintered as we went through it.

Pain shot through me as I landed heavily on the broken wood, causing me to cry out. He drew back a fist and hit me flush in the face causing more stars to appear.

Ignoring the pain, I rolled to the right, throwing him clear. With a grimace on my face, I came up to my knees and then lurched to my feet. The bodyguard followed suit and charged at me. He hit me low in the middle and drove me backwards. I brought a fist down on the back of his neck, stunning him, dropping him to his knees. I hit him again and again. Grabbing a handful of hair, I lifted his head up so his face was looking at me before I hit him flush in the jaw. The bodyguard went limp and slumped to the floor.

I looked up and saw Palmer making a beeline to the fallen gun on the floor. He bent down and scooped it up, bringing it level to fire.

I dived for my own weapon, grabbed it, lifted it, and fired three times. With each bullet strike, Palmer rose onto the balls of his feet, rigid as a board.

Blood flowed from the holes and his shirt started to turn red. He dropped to the floor and lay still.

I glanced at Alice who was frozen in shock. I said to her, "We have to get out of here. Now."

Alice followed me out the door into the hallway. People were starting to gather as they came out of their rooms to see what the commotion was all about. Using the uniform I wore to my advantage, I called out, "Everybody, return to your rooms. We have a situation, and you will all be safer there."

By the time we reached the elevator, the hallway was clear once more as everybody had disappeared hurriedly back into their rooms.

A few minutes later, we were traversing the lobby, rushing towards the main entrance, where, once outside, an awaiting laundry van would whisk us away.

***

"Well, that's that then," I growled in frustration at the failure of the operation.

Clark was optimistic. "Not true, Kane, not true. If anything, the operation was successful, even if you didn't get Palmer alive. He's dead, out of the picture and the conglomerate is headless."

"What will you do now?"

"Watch them. Keep an eye on their activities. Make sure that they can't get up to too much trouble. The director of the CIA has given me the go ahead to form a new section that will be dedicated solely to them. In fact, I've been asked to offer you a job. If you wish to come to work for us."

I was stunned. I didn't know what to say. "Why me?"

"Because you're good at what you do, and you don't give up even when the odds are stacked against you. And you do whatever it takes to complete your mission."

I looked at Alice, who was smiling at me. "What do you think?"

"I think you should take it."

"Who's going to be in charge of this team?" I asked Clark.

"I will be," he replied. "Mind you, we've still got a lot to clean up before we get started."

I thought about it for a moment before looking at Alice again and then I gave a nod. "I'll do it."

THE PRESENT...

Kane closed the book and lay it on his lap. He looked up, digesting what he'd read over the past couple of days. He had two big questions which remained unanswered. Who was the old man he'd met in Hong Kong? And who were these people he was dealing with now?

There was movement at the entrance of the warehouse, and Kane looked up to see three people enter through the open door.

One was Peters, the other was Sara. The third he'd never seen before. It was a man with fair hair and narrow eyes.

Kane stood up and tucked the diary inside his shirt. Sara said to him, "There's someone here to see you, John."

Abbott had appeared, and Kane immediately became tense. His weapon was within reach at the small of his back. Kane stared at the man and nodded. "Howdy."

"At last, we meet, Mr. Kane. My name is Craig Palmer."

Suddenly, everything began to fall into place. Everything had been a setup, a well-oiled pantomime.

"I can see by the expression on your face that you have questions. Ask away."

When Kane glanced at Abbott again, he could see that the man had his weapon out. But he wasn't alone. Now the rest of his team had joined him. "This was a mighty elaborate ruse to get to me."

"And worth every part of it," Palmer said.

"Maybe you should just go ahead and tell me everything instead of me asking questions and you drip-feeding me the information. Start with the old man who was meant to be my father's friend who actually died in 1968."

He saw the expression on Peters's face change and mouth a curse word.

Palmer raised his eyebrows. "The diary?"

"Yes, the diary. If it even is true, whatever I read in it?"

"Yes, Mr. Kane. The diary is true. It was taken from your grandfather the day he boarded that plane by my father. You see, this whole thing is a family vendetta. Only you and your sister are left. Your grandfather killed my grandfather. My father killed your grandfather, your father and your mother. Your grandmother was already dead by then."

Kane was stunned by the news. He frowned, his mind taking over as a million things ran through it.

Palmer said, "I see you're still thinking that your father had a heart attack and died behind the wheel, killing your mother as well. Well, he kind of did have a heart attack, but it was helped along by, let's just say something he ingested. Your sister was meant to have died in that crash too, but she didn't, and you, well you were deployed overseas. But now it's time.

The honor has fallen to me."

"Who was the old man?" Kane asked.

"Just someone we hired to play the part."

"How did he know so much about my grandfather?"

"By reading all the information we had that was given to him. But apparently, he was becoming too painful, untrustworthy. So Sara asked for permission to have him eliminated. It was going to happen sooner or later, so I didn't care one way or the other."

This was what the old man was trying to warn him about.

Kane's anger was rising within him, and he fought to keep it under control. But he still had a couple more questions. "What happened to the conglomerate?"

Palmer grinned. "Nothing. We're still out there. Still influencing the government and making policy as we had done it back in the 60s. It doesn't matter who is leading the country; they all bend to our will. They may think they run the country, but in fact, it's us that make the policy."

What a psycho fuck. Kane still had another question. "Why are the Kowloon Triad after me?"

"Because your grandfather killed Ling."

"You know you have a traitor amongst your people, don't you?" Kane said.

Palmer stared passively at him, no emotion showing on his face.

Kane continued, "Everywhere we've been, the triad has popped up. The only way they can know where we are is if somebody is telling them. That means somebody here is feeding them information.

Do you trust any of them, Palmer?"

"I trust everyone that works for me, Mr. Kane," he said unmoved.

"Then if I was you, I'd think again."

Suddenly the air was ripped apart by flying bullets and the sound of automatic weapon fire. Kane dived for the floor as one of Abbott's men died under a storm of bullets. Shouts filled the warehouse as armed men stormed in.

They were Asian; had to be Triad.

Abbott opened fire with his own weapon and an attacker fell; a cry of pain escaping his lips.

Kane looked about trying to ascertain the biggest threat. He took out his P226 and paused. They seemed more intent on killing each other.

A high-pitched cry drew his attention. "There! He's over there!"

He expected Sara to be pointing in his direction, but she wasn't. Instead, she was pointing directly at Palmer, screeching at the top of her voice. "Well, I guess we know who the traitor was."

"Fucking bitch!" Peters cried out. "You stinking, traitorous whore."

Peters brought up his handgun and fired twice. Both bullets punched into Sara as she was unaware of her immediate threat. Kane saw her fall to the hard floor, her body twisting in pain.

The gunfire seemed to intensify as more triad members appeared. But Abbott and his team were well trained and met the threat head on.

All around Kane men were dying. The air was filled with bullets and the roar of guns. Glancing about for somewhere to hide, Kane saw Palmer out of the corner of his eye as he exited the building through an open doorway. "Not today, Josephine. You're mine."

Kane came to his feet and ran across the warehouse while bullets zipped all around him. A triad shooter appeared in front of him, and he fired at point blank range. The shooter staggered under the impact and Kane pushed him aside.

Meanwhile the two sides fought a vicious battle for supremacy in the confines of the warehouse.

Abbott dropped to a knee as he took a bullet in the thigh. However, far from putting him out of the fight, he killed the triad man who'd shot him. Peters on the other hand wasn't so lucky. A hailstorm of slugs hammered into his chest from a sub-machine gun wielded by one of the triad shooters.

Kane disappeared out through the door hot on the heels of Palmer. He saw the man vanish through some bushes thick enough to hide his flight.

The man called Reaper hit them at speed and burst through to the other side. Ahead of him was Palmer, still fleeing for his life. "Stop there, Palmer!" Kane shouted.

But the man kept running. Kane knew if he got away that he would come again. He may not be able to stop the conglomerate, but he could certainly hurt them.

He raised his gun and fired.

Palmer threw out his arms and fell forward. Kane walked over to him and looked down. The fallen man rolled over and looked up at his assailant. The bullet had hit him low down and exited through the front, soaking his shirt in blood.

Kane said, "You know what they say about the best laid plans and all."

"Go ahead," Palmer sneered, pain in his voice. "Do it."

Kane had gone through hell bringing the Cabal to its knees and now the last thing he needed was another clandestine organization lurking in the shadows. "How many of you?"

Bracing himself to be shot, Palmer was suddenly confused. "What?"

"The conglomerate. How many?"

He spat at Kane, "Screw you."

Kane shrugged. "It was worth a shot." Then he killed him.

Looking at the dead man, Kane realized that the shooting had stopped. He turned and looked back at the trees which blocked out the view of the warehouse. He knew he shouldn't, but he did. Kane checked the loads in his P226 and started walking back the way he'd come.

***

It seemed like everyone in the warehouse was dead. Triad shooters were scattered across the floor. Sara was dead, a mask of pain etched on her face. Peters too lay in a large pool of blood. Abbott's men were all down, including their leader. It was a complete bloodbath.

"I see we still have one alive." The voice echoed throughout the cavernous building.

Kane turned and saw two men walking towards him. One was wounded. Both were armed. He said, "You paid a high price for this, Quan."

The Triad leader paused, surprised.

"You know who I am?"

"Wild guess," Kane replied.

"Who are you?"

"John Kane. My friends call me Reaper."

Recognition flared in his eyes. Then he nodded. "The man everyone wants to kill."

"It seems to be a trend. How about you? I heard you wanted me too. Something about my grandfather killing yours."

Quan shrugged. "Maybe another time, perhaps. Right now, I'm after someone else."

"Palmer?"

"Yes."

"He's dead."

The triad boss looked puzzled. "You know this because?"

"I just killed him."

"I see."

Kane said, "You know I'm going to come after you, right? Even if you let me go, I'll be coming."

Quan nodded. "Maybe—"

BANG! BANG! BANG!

The triad boss dropped with three rounds from Kane's P226 in his chest. He hit the ground hard, his eyes open, staring at the roof of the warehouse. A pool of blood started to grow around him, dark and rich.

Kane turned his attention to the wounded man who just stood there looking down at his boss. He looked up at the man called Reaper and his jaw dropped. "No!"

"Nothing personal," Kane said, and shot him too.

Kane felt a wave of relief flood over him. It was all over. Then he found himself thinking of his grandfather, his parents. The diary had told him so much but ultimately it had also told him nothing. He never knew who his grandfather and grandmother were. And then to find out about the deaths of his parents in such a brutal way, it felt all too much.

But now that he knew that the conglomerate was still out there, he couldn't let it go. His grandfather wouldn't have, and neither would he. He'd find them one day, unless they found him first.

Kane reached into his pocket for his cell. He punched in a number and waited for it to be answered. "Yeah, I need a ride."

A LOOK AT THE WOLF'S TREASURE: A BROOKE REYNOLDS AND MARK BUTLER STORY

Treasure Book One

Brooke Reynolds had once been an integral part of Team Reaper. Now, she's taking on a new kind of mission...

The Schmidt Foundation is hellbent on finding and restoring a priceless treasure worth more than is imaginable, accrued by the Nazis during the second great war. They seek to return this priceless artifact to its rightful place.

But when their strongest lead culminates in the death of one of their own on the shores of Lake Toplitz, Johann Schmidt turns to the two people he knows can help the Foundation find it—Brooke Reynolds and their fallen's son, Mark Butler.

Together, Brooke and Mark traverse the globe—armed killers snarling at their heels—looking for what could be the greatest treasure known to man. And at its pinnacle? The most coveted jewel in the crown...the long thought lost Amber Room.

AVAILABLE ON AMAZON

ABOUT THE AUTHOR

A relative newcomer to the world of writing, Brent Towns self-published his first book, a western, in 2015. *Last Stand in Sanctuary* took him two years to write. His first hardcover book, a Black Horse Western, was published the following year.

Since then, he has written 26 western stories, including some in collaboration with British western author, Ben Bridges.

Also, he has written the novelization to the upcoming 2019 movie from One-Eyed Horse Productions, titled, *Bill Tilghman and the Outlaws*. Not bad for an Australian author, he thinks.

Brent Towns has also scripted three Commando Comics with another two to come.

He says, "The obvious next step for me was to venture into the world of men's action/adventure/thriller stories. Thus, Team Reaper was born."

A country town in Queensland, Australia, is where Brent lives with his wife and son.

In the past, he worked as a seaweed factory worker, a knife-hand in an abattoir, mowed lawns and tidied gardens, worked in caravan parks, and worked in the hire industry. And now, as well as writing books, Brent is a home tutor for his son doing distance education.

Brent's love of reading used to take over his life, now it's writing that does that; often sitting up until the small hours, bashing away at his tortured keyboard where he loses himself in the world of fiction.